Marike stopped talking and closed her eyes, sighing. "Are you convinced I'm real?" she asked softly.

"Yes," Gail said. "I think I am. But perhaps it doesn't matter. If this is a dream, we're both in it." She smiled, tracing the outline of Marike's lips. "But I have to admit you feel real to me."

Marike kissed Gail's fingertips and rolled on her side to face her. She raised a hand to stroke Gail's hair, then put her hand against Gail's cheek. Gail closed her eyes. It all seemed so *right*. And suddenly she knew what she wanted.

"Make love to me, Marike," she whispered.

"Are you sure?"

"I'm sure." And she was. Absolutely. She took Marike's hand from her cheek, turned it over, and kissed the palm. Marike murmured and, emboldened, Gail leaned over and pressed her mouth to Marike's. It felt strange to take the lead, but exciting, too. "I'm sure," she repeated. Sensing the other woman's hesitance, she brushed her lips across Marike's again, feeling the gentle pressure as Marike responded.

Osten's Bay

Zenobia N. Vole

NAIAD
1988

Printed in the United States of America
First Edition

Edited by Katherine V. Forrest and Cecil Dawkins
Cover design by Pat Tong and Bonnie Liss
   (Phoenix Graphics)
Typesetting by Sandi Stancil

Library of Congress Cataloging-in-Publication Data

   Vole, Zenobia N.
   Osten's Bay / Zenobia N. Vole
       p.   cm.
   ISBN 0-941483-15-0 : $8.95
   I. Title.
PS3572.03708 1988   87-31180
813'.54--dc 19   CIP

For Martha:
Alexi's best friend,
and mine, too.

ABOUT THE AUTHOR

Zenobia N. Vole was born of Burmese parents in Las Vegas, Nevada, an event which she has always considered auspicious. She was educated in Las Vegas and completed training in her craft in Tucson, Arizona. Shortly thereafter she moved to Southern California where she now lives with her lifetime partner, Alexi. She feels that her early training in Oriental philosophy — particularly meditation — has proved invaluable in her work. When not on the word processor, she can be found birdwatching or engaged in photography.

Prologue

The woman stood in a pool of moonlight beside Gail's bed. Through the open window behind her the surf made a soft, entreating sound, a murmur like a sigh repeated. The woman reached out a hand, and with no hesitation, Gail took it. The woman's face was as familiar to Gail as her own, and yet her mind could not supply a name. Somehow, that seemed unimportant — Gail knew this woman well. Hand in hand, they walked together out of the cabin and into the soft summer night.

Out on the beach, the sound of the surf was louder, more insistent. The tide was coming in, and the sea caressed their feet with eager waves as warm as blood. A pale, luminous moon hung just above the horizon, and in its light everything was silver and black, chiaroscuro, magical. A dreamscape. The woman turned. Her eyes shone like gems and her hair was the color of moonlight.

The woman raised Gail's hand to her face and kissed her palm with lips as soft as moth's wings. Gail shivered. The woman touched Gail's face gently, tracing the outline of eyebrows, cheekbones, nose, mouth.

The incoming tide now boiled around their calves, and the woman took Gail's hand and led her up the beach, beyond the high tide line. She knelt in a black patch of shadow beneath a trio of towering palms and ran warm hands over the backs of Gail's bare thighs. Eyes shining, she held out her hands to Gail. Suddenly, as she leaned out into the moonlight, arms raised, eyes shadowed, she appeared much more than flesh and blood woman. Washed in silver light, she was symbol, archetype, a figure charged with meaning. Surely Gail had seen such images on the faces of old coins, or on temple walls, drawing down the moon's power — warriors, priestesses, hunters. Awestruck, Gail stared, suddenly aware that she was in the presence of some ancient mystery, something that had bound women together down through the ages, connecting their souls like silver beads on a string. Something invisible, yet so potent that it frightened men and daunted weaker women. Something, she realized, that also included her.

Stunned by this revelation, she stood motionless for a moment like an eternity. Then, a little frightened, she reached for the woman in front of her, needing to affirm the corporeal, living, real presence.

A cloud scudded across the face of the moon, plunging the world into darkness. Blind, disoriented, Gail called out ... and awoke sitting up in bed, in a cheap hotel room in Aruba, alone. "No!" she said, a terrible feeling of loss overcoming her.

She switched on the light, half expecting to find the woman lying in bed beside her, or standing by the window. But there was no one there. She shivered, and drew the sheet up to her neck. Unwilling to relinquish the dream — for surely, that was what it had been — she closed her eyes, trying to recapture it. But already the woman's features, her hair, the shape of her hands, were fading from Gail's memory. A wave of anguish and despair broke over her, and against her will, she began to sob. "Why?" she called out, uncertain of the content of the question, or even the entity to whom she should direct it. Feeling cheated and baffled, she put her head in her arms and wept.

After a few moments, she wiped her eyes and poured herself a Scotch. Walking to the window, she held the torn curtain aside and stood looking at the flashing red neon sign across the hotel parking lot. A small, hot breeze ruffled her hair and for one moment she remembered cool nighttime sea air on her skin and the feel of a woman's touch on her lips. She swallowed the rest of her drink in one gulp, turned out the light, and climbed back into bed. Erotic dreams of women might be fine for others, but not for her. She frowned, remembering: hadn't she put all that behind her with Janice's departure? Loving — and perhaps loving women in particular — meant misunderstanding, pain, tears, and regret. No, no matter how she might be tempted, such things weren't for her. She was a scientist, a seeker after rational truths, a lover

3

of order. Relinquishing self control led, invariably, to disaster. Did she want to be governed by emotion? Hardly. She had abandoned such a life; she had no desire to experience its chaos again. Firmly closing her eyes, she willed herself to sleep.

Chapter 1

Gail Murray descended the steps of the Antillean Airlines plane and winced as the heat on the runway struck her like a blow. Some distance ahead — much farther than she wanted to walk in this August heat — the terminal of Bonaire's one airport beckoned like an oasis. She walked purposefully toward it, heedless of the calls of the plane's co-pilot who had unloaded her bags onto the runway and was exhorting her to carry them indoors. To hell with you, she fumed. I had to spend last night in a sleazy hotel in Aruba because your crummy airline was on a work slowdown; I'm a day late starting my new job; and I haven't had a shower or any breakfast. The least you can do for me is carry my bloody bags.

Inside the terminal building, the temperature was at least twenty degrees cooler. That makes it about one hundred, Gail thought testily, licking a moustache of sweat off her upper lip. She stood for a while in the relative cool of the terminal, looking around in disapproval. No one seemed to be working. Two men Gail took for baggage handlers lounged near a motionless conveyor belt; several clerks at the ticket counter looked drugged; and the few passengers waiting for their flights seemed unconscious. Gail yawned. The heat was getting to her, too, even at ten in the morning. She remembered what ISAUR's director had told her: "Call the Institute as soon as you get in and we'll send someone for you. Don't even think about taking a cab." She looked around for a phone. Nothing.

The baggage conveyor belt started up, lurched convulsively, and spilled two blue nylon diving bags into the terminal. Her baggage. Well, some of it, anyway. She roused herself from her stupor and walked toward them. At that moment, a slim young blond man in a pair of faded, cut-off jeans, a once pink T-shirt that read BE KIND TO ANIMALS: KISS A SHARK, sunglasses, and a white cloth cyclist's cap, unfolded himself from where he had been lounging against the wall near the conveyor belt and reached for Gail's baggage. For a moment Gail just stared, her mouth open. She couldn't believe the cool nonchalance this scruffy young thief displayed as he was about to make off with her baggage. In broad daylight, too. It was the last straw.

"Hey, you," Gail said angrily, hurrying up to him and grabbing one of the blue bags. "Those are my bags, dammit. Keep your hands off them."

The young man turned in amazement.

"And don't look so innocent, buddy," Gail told him. "You were about to take those bags, weren't you?"

The would-be thief took off his sunglasses and let them dangle from the cord around his neck. "As a matter of fact, I was," he said calmly, blinking eyelashes so pale blond they looked white. His eyes were an astonishing mossy green and looked, in his tanned face, like precious stones. Emeralds. No man deserves to have such pretty eyes, Gail thought, as angry with his beauty as with his irritatingly calm demeanor. "Look," he said, bending to show Gail the baggage tags.

Gail Looked. "Marike Osten, Osten's Bay, Bonaire, Dutch West Indies," she read aloud. "But ... but ..." she stammered weakly, feeling like a fool. "So who's Marike Osten," she asked, to cover her embarrassment.

"Not Mar-*eek*-a," the young man said, correcting her pronunciation. "*Mar*-ick-a." He smiled in amusement. "Like America without the A. And incidentally, I'm Marike."

Marike. A woman's name. Gail wished the floor would open up and swallow her. Not only had she called this young woman a thief, she'd mistaken her for a boy. She looked more closely and saw a woman of about forty, tall, tanned, and slim. "Oh, hell," she said weakly. "I'm sorry. I —" She shrugged. "I feel like an idiot, but my diving bags look just like those. The ALM co-pilot left them on the runway. I thought someone had brought them inside."

Marike shook her head. "Not likely. During the work slowdown tourists have to carry their own."

"Oh? You didn't have to carry yours."

Marike smiled enigmatically. "Ah, but I'm not a tourist. I live here. We natives take care of each other."

7

She took off her cap and ran a hand through her short, blond hair. It had been tucked behind her ears, but sprang aggressively into curls as Marike combed it with her fingers. Noticing Gail's eyes on her, she jammed the cap firmly back on her head. "Hot," she commented, giving the bill of the cap a decisive tug. "Well, let's see about your bags."

But Gail was staring at Marike, thinking how fine and soft her hair looked, and not listening to a thing she'd been saying.

"Your bags," Marike repeated. "I bet they're roasting out there on the runway. I'll help you get them if you like."

"All right," Gail said in a daze. What *is* the matter with you, she asked herself. This woman is trying to be kind. If you can't seem grateful, at least pay attention.

"Brother," Marike said as they walked together out to the runway, blinking in the relentless sunlight. "I hope you brought lots of sunscreen."

"Oh yes. Sunscreen," Gail said, wrenching her thoughts away from Marike's eyes and hair. "I think I brought enough."

Marike took one of Gail's diving bags in each hand, leaving Gail two suitcases to carry. "Planning a long stay?" she asked grinning. "Or are you like me — afraid to leave anything behind?"

"A little of both," Gail said, uncomfortably aware of how close together they were walking. Finally they were back inside the terminal.

Marike deposited Gail's bags on the floor, wiped her palms on her cutoffs, and looked at her watch. She gave her cap another tug, looking uncomfortable. "Well, I'd better get going." She hesitated a moment. "I have to go north, up the coast. Otherwise I'd give you a lift to hotel alley. Sorry." She picked up her own diving bags. "Listen," she said, "if you want to do some real diving — you know, see some things that your hotel dive package won't include — come on up to Osten's Bay."

"What kinds of things?" Gail asked, glad to have something else to say to Marike. Standing in the hot, stuffy terminal talking to this woman suddenly seemed like the most appealing thing in the world.

"Sea turtles. Caves. Sleeping sharks."

"You're a pretty good PR woman for Osten's Bay," Gail told her. "Do you work there?"

Marike smiled, an unreadable expression on her face. "In a manner of speaking."

Probably the owner's daughter, Gail thought. Or his niece. Or, worse yet, his wife. This thought bothered her, and she put it promptly out of her mind. "I'll think about it," Gail said. And suddenly there was nothing else to say. "Thanks for your help with the bags," she concluded lamely.

"No problem," Marike said. She looked at Gail for another moment, then turned and walked out of the terminal. Gail watched the other woman walk all the way to the door, unable to take her eyes off Marike's long legs, her tanned arms, the jaunty white cap, her retreating back.

Chapter 2

After finally locating a phone and making a call to the Institute, Gail spent an additional five frustrating minutes finding the bathroom. She gave one of the porters a dollar to watch her two diving bags and large suitcase, and took her smallest bag with her. Filling one of the basins with cold water, she washed her face, then decided that she would do what she could to get cool. What did she care who came into the washroom and saw her taking a bath in the basin? She peeled off her once crisp white cotton slacks and blue chambray shirt and dug a pair of khaki shorts and a green Erindale College polo shirt out of her bag. Standing there in her underwear, she washed her face and hands and splashed water on her arms and the back of her neck. Already she felt better.

Drying herself with paper towels, she looked critically in the mirror. Gail Murray. Brown hair, grey eyes, a sprinkling of freckles across her nose. Neither tall nor short, pretty nor plain. She made a face at herself. Her mother used to describe her as wholesome and outdoorsy-looking; her ex-husband Allan, as healthy; her lover Janice, as androgynous. She frowned. At least people no longer referred to her as tomboyish. Now they just called her athletic-looking. A polite euphemism.

She ran a comb through her fine wavy hair and decided that, as soon as she was settled at the Institute, she would have it cut. SCUBA diving, and Bonaire's intolerable summer humidity, definitely called for short hair. She combed it behind her ears and shook her head in disapproval. Athletic or tomboyish, long hair or short, she would never win a beauty contest. She would never be half as good looking as, well, as that woman Marike, for instance.

Disturbed, she brought the comb down away from her hair. Again she saw Marike unfold herself, stretch, and walk to the baggage conveyor belt. She remembered the tanned, strong legs, the capable hands, the confident set of her shoulders. Gail's eyes were drawn to the mirror, to her own image, and for a moment she saw not her own hair but the fine curly blond hair that had sprung up when Marike removed her cap. And instead of her own rather ordinary grey eyes, she saw Marike's green ones. She blinked and the image was gone.

Shivering a little, she rubbed her arms and put her comb away. Come off it, Gail, she chastised herself. You're here to do a job, to work. Stop this preoccupation with

11

your appearance. Men won't be interested in you even if you were interested in them. You just send them the wrong signals. Remember Allan? It didn't take him long to decide he'd made a mistake. And what about Janice? She wasn't interested for long either. Face it, kid, you're neither attractive nor desirable. What you've got going for you are your brains. So use them.

Setting her lips in a grim line, she folded her good clothes and tucked them away in her bag, quickly dressing in her shorts and polo shirt. She dragged an old pair of Reeboks out of her bag and jammed her feet into them, lacing them quickly. There. She was ready.

Retrieving her bags from the dozing porter, she stood at the doorway of the terminal, looking off down the road for the Institute's jeep. After a few minutes, her thoughts turned to the job she had been hired to do here on Bonaire. Her field of research was underwater geology — a specialty that let her combine her love of the ocean and SCUBA diving with her passion for geology. But so far, she had to admit ruefully, she hadn't exactly set the world on fire. Here she was at thirty-three, five years after receiving her doctorate, still stuck at the same small college in Canada from which she'd graduated. True, Erindale College was a campus of the prestigious University of Toronto, but grant money was drying up everywhere. Being affiliated with a big university didn't help a bit. Her particular research project — the development of a computer program to predict the location of cavities in coral reefs — just hadn't excited anyone. Oh, she had had two small papers published in the *Journal of Sedimentary Petrology,* but no one had paid any attention to them. And she hadn't had the opportunity to gather any new research data in over a

12

year. Her project was standing still. So when Benjamin Sloat, reclusive director of the world-famous Institute for South Atlantic Undersea Research had approached her and offered her a job, she had jumped at the chance. But now she wasn't so sure that she had made a sensible decision.

First of all, there was the fact that so little was known about ISAUR. It regularly produced stacks of research papers on all aspects of marine science, but when she tried, she couldn't find anyone who had ever worked there. Then there was the vagueness of her job description. What exactly did they want her to do? The letter offering her the job had been maddeningly sketchy, and her subsequent letters asking for clarification had gone virtually unanswered. Finally, Dr. Sloat had scribbled his name on a blank contract and appended a Post-It note saying "Just make your computer program work. Write your own job description. I'll agree. Sign and return the contract."

She shook her head. Dr. Sloat might have had no clear idea of what she was to do at the Institute, but he certainly had a crystal clear idea of how much she was worth. The check accompanying the telegram, representing her first month's salary in advance, had stunned her. It was twice her monthly salary at Erindale. That, at least, hadn't been vague. It had spoken eloquently. As soon as the funds had cleared her bank and been deposited in her savings account, she had signed the contract and returned it to ISAUR. And she had stopped worrying about things like job descriptions.

Her stomach rumbled and she looked at her watch. Where was that damned ride?

* * * * *

When the Institute's jeep pulled up in front of the passenger terminal over an hour later, she was hot, hungry, thirsty, and more irritable than ever. She gave the driver of the jeep — a gangly young redhead with a terrible sunburn — a particularly foul look as he heaved her bags into the back and motioned her toward the passenger seat.

"I'm Russ McGinnis," he said, extending his hand, oblivious to her bad mood. He held the door for her with exaggerated courtesy, grinning. "See, chivalry isn't dead after all. Oh, I know that divers carry their own gear — even women divers — but Dr. Sloat explained to me in excruciating detail what he'd do if I didn't roll out the red carpet for you. And, as you'll be my boss," he looked at her sidelong, "I have my own reasons for wanting to give you a decent welcome."

She couldn't help smiling a little at Russ's good humor, and she could see the young man relax. "I'm Gail Murray," she told him, "but I guess you already know that. What do you mean, I'll be your boss? I thought I'd be working alone, in the computer facility. Do you work there?"

Russ snorted. "I sure don't. I'm just a flunkey — a marine biology doctoral candidate. No, I'm afraid some crazy things are going on at ISAUR. My diving buddies and I heard through the grapevine that you were coming, and I got nominated to brief you on a few things before you see Sloat." He hurried to explain. "I'm not a meddler, Dr. Murray. What I have to tell you is for all our sakes."

"So tell me," she said, mystified.

"First of all, you'll be my boss because Sloat has picked you to be our team's divemaster. Obviously this is news to you."

14

Gail was incredulous. "He did what?"

Russ nodded. "Yeah. Welcome to ISAUR. Every day brings a new adventure."

"I can't believe this," she said.

"Believe it. And something else you should believe is that Sloat couldn't give that job away."

"Why not?"

"Two divemasters have quit in the last two months. Now the native divers — the ones who do the donkey work — say our team is jinxed. They won't dive with us. And Sloat couldn't find anyone qualified who wanted the job. Except you."

"I certainly don't want it," Gail said heatedly.

"I don't see how you can get out of it," Russ told her. "Once ISAUR has you, you find yourself doing all kinds of things you never bargained for. We're a lot like indentured servants here."

"Well, you could always leave."

Russ shook his head. "Nope. I need Sloat's blessing. With his recommendation, and this experience, I can get a job in my field anywhere in the world. If I blow it here at ISAUR, I can kiss my future goodbye."

Gail sighed. Russ was right.

"But cheer up. Think of the bonus," Russ told her.

"What bonus?" she asked, feeling absurdly like a character who had wandered onto the wrong movie set. She certainly didn't know these lines.

Russ laughed a little bitterly. "Yeah, I forgot. You wouldn't know anything about the bonuses Dr. Sloat is offering. Hell, he didn't even ask you to be divemaster. Say, would you like to go some place cool and have lunch and a beer? It will mean being late for your appointment with Sloat, but maybe we should talk some more."

"I'd certainly like some lunch," she told Russ. "And a beer wouldn't hurt either. Maybe Dr. Sloat can wait a little longer."

* * * * *

On the shaded balcony of the Atlantis Hotel, Gail poured herself a glass of Amstel beer and took a few grateful swallows. The waitress fussed over Russ, evidently a regular, finally bringing them a plate of somewhat dry chicken salad sandwiches. She batted her eyes at Russ, lingering and chatting, and pointedly ignoring Gail, who fervently wished she would disappear. She finally turned her attention to the sandwiches. Ravenous, she ate three, then gazed off across the bay, sipping her beer while the waitress talked with Russ.

Just below the restaurant's balcony, the turquoise water was so clear she could see stands of brown and green elkhorn coral close to the surface. A perfect spot to snorkel, she thought, noting the easy access from the beach and the numerous clear spaces underwater between stands of coral.

"Sorry," Russ said, breaking into her thoughts. Gail looked around to discover they were alone. "It's not that I like Zoe," he told her, "but she's a useful contact. She works with the hotel's catering department and hears the most amazing things."

"I hardly know where to start asking questions," Gail said. "And you probably aren't the person who could answer them, anyhow."

Russ shrugged. "I could speculate."

"Hmmm," Gail said doubtfully. "I'm beginning to like Dr. Sloat less and less. It's a little unbelievable that he didn't write to me about being divemaster. My last communication from the Institute — well, from his secretary, Miss Liszt — was really about administrative matters. Apparently she was setting up my file — getting ready for me to download my data from Erindale's computer to the computer at the Institute. She needed to know how much space to allocate, she said. I gave her Erindale's codes so she could look at the size of my data file. Also, she wanted to know the databases I'd be using so she could get me access passwords — that sort of thing. No mention was made of taking on an additional duty, or of any bonus. I assumed I'd just be working on the Institute's computer program for locating coral reef cavities." She shook her head. "I just don't understand it."

Russ swallowed the last of his beer and began to shred the bottle's label. "Well, he's not being straight with you. But if he didn't bother to tell you you'd be divemaster, well, why bother to tell you anything else?"

"Tell me about the bonuses," Gail said.

Russ shrugged. "Why not? They're no secret. The team that's the first to use the new computer program to find cavities gets a ten thousand dollar bonus." He looked uncomfortable. "But here's another thing you should know. This terrific computer program — if it exists — is a joke. Toshio, my diving buddy, thinks Sloat throws darts at those photographic blowups of reefs hanging on his office wall, then makes the diving assignments." He shook his head. "Toshio's somewhat irreverent, but he might be right, judging from the success we've had." He looked quickly up at her, then resumed shredding his beer bottle label. "It's odd, but for reasons known only to the good doctor, he wants us to think the computer is spewing out the diving assignments. Maybe he figures we'll have more confidence if a machine gives us our instructions. I don't know."

Gail shook her head, puzzled. "What cavity location program? I didn't think the Institute had one. At least not a viable program — nothing that worked. That's why Dr. Sloat hired me. And he sure couldn't have developed something so complex in three months. Or could he?" She ran a hand through her hair. "What's going on here?"

"Beats me," Russ said.

She was silent for a few minutes, trying to make sense out of all this. She gave up. "There's only one person who can answer my questions. Dr. Sloat."

Russ snorted. "If he will. He used to be a half decent human being, but lately he's unbearable. I think his job's riding on this cavity location thing." He dug in the pocket of his shorts and counted out money to pay the bill. As she stood up to leave, he put a hand on her arm. She turned to him. "Listen," he said, "there's one more thing. If you're anything like the rest of us, you'll do what Sloat wants. You'll be our divemaster. I don't know what's going on at ISAUR with this cavity program, and I don't care. But what I — we — do care about is our skins. I don't want to seem melodramatic, but we'd like to end our tour here in one piece. Oh sure, we'd like to share in the bonus, don't get me wrong, but we can live without it. Our last divemaster, Jan Voorman, was a real slavedriver. Toshio got the bends twice because Voorman made mistakes using the diving tables. He was careless. And he worked us like dogs — something you just can't do with divers. We need to know what kind of boss you're likely to be, Dr. Murray."

Gail understood. "Assuming that I take the job as divemaster," she told him, "you can be sure of two things. One: I won't put your lives in jeopardy. I don't make

18

mistakes working the diving tables. And two: I'll expect you to do what you're told. To do your jobs. That's all. Oh, and I couldn't care less about the bonus. All right?"

Russ nodded. "All right. And thanks."

* * * * *

As the jeep sped along the coast road to the Institute, she wondered what to make of the things Russ had told her — her unwelcome job of divemaster, the bonuses, the Institute's computer program. She shook her head. It was the last point that worried her most. How was it possible that the Institute now had a viable (well, almost) computer program? Who had developed it? As far as she knew, hers was the only such research project in existence. And what about the Institute's program — would it be compatible with hers? Who would be in charge — she, or the mysterious programmer? And why had she been kept in the dark about this? She found herself beginning to get very angry and decided to put these things out of her mind until she reached the Institute. By then she would have cooled down — a necessary condition for discussing possible breach of contract. She would not play the emotional female with Benjamin Sloat.

She turned her thoughts to what she had read about the island paradise that would be her home for the next year. A nineteen mile long island in the Dutch Antilles, no more than twenty miles from the coast of South America, Bonaire was a SCUBA diver's paradise. Over the years she'd read enough diving copy filed from Bonaire to convince herself that she almost knew the place. Fabulous, enchanting, spellbinding, the articles said, and from what she had seen of the offshore reefs, she had no reason to disagree. This sedate little island with its stubby hills and craggy coastline seemed to have all the attributes of paradise. Its reefs were healthy and vibrant. Water clarity was extraordinary, and colors took on a hard, sharp, edge. Marine life was abundant. One of the rules for divers was to feed the fish every chance they got. She smiled. That would make for a very congenial relationship.

And dive sites were apparently endless. Unlike other islands where there was a theme and variations, Bonaire's strong suit was its variety. There were walls, and the intriguing double reefs at Angel City, and the fabled mystery wreck. And unlike other islands where it was usually necessary to take a dive boat out half a mile to the reef, Bonaire's reefs were accessible from most beaches. You simply needed to put on your tanks and wade into the sea. She couldn't wait for some time off so she could visit the dive sites at her leisure.

They drove up a steep hill, and from its crest she could see a little bay gleaming in the noon sun. At the water's edge, huddling on the rocky shore, was a cluster of buildings and docks. Most of the buildings were white stucco with red tile roofs, but a group of them sat apart at the water's edge, looking for all the world like enormous ping pong balls.

"There it is," Russ told her. "The Institute for South Atlantic Undersea Research — ISAUR."

"What are those odd-looking round buildings?" Gail asked.

"ISAUR's newest additions," Russ answered in disgust. "Have you ever seen anything like them? Right out of a science fiction movie." He shook his head again. "They're geodesic domes. Held up by air pressure apparently. They were Sloat's idea — he had them put up about a year ago." Russ shook his head again. "God, they're ugly. Sloat put the arm on some rich resource company, and they coughed up a grant for the Institute. I guess these buildings were part of the deal. They're experimental, apparently. And our benefactors installed a whole new computer system, too. Look there." Russ pointed to a spot about a hundred yards away from the largest dome. "Even gave us a helicopter. And built that heliport. Impressive, isn't it?"

"Who is this benefactor?" Gail wondered, thinking wistfully of what her little college could have done with such money.

"A natural resource company," Russ said. "DARDCO, I think they're called." He shrugged. "Business is not exactly the scientist's best friend, but Sloat thinks it will work out." He laughed. "Obviously he hasn't read the story of Faust."

Russ maneuvered the jeep between a pair of tall pillars that held a sign identifying the Institute in English, Dutch, and Spanish. A little parking lot in front of a pair of substantial white stucco buildings held a few Institute vehicles, a bevy of motor scooters, and some ancient Japanese compact cars. "I'll be down on the dock when you're done," Russ said. "You'll need someone to show you where you'll be living. To get to Sloat's office, though, just walk between these buildings and take the flagstone path to your right. It will bring you down to the beach were the domes are. Sloat's office is clearly marked. Good luck," he said, forcing a smile.

"Thanks," Gail told him, feeling like a tardy pupil about to meet the school principal.

* * * * *

21

Benjamin Sloat's office was not hard to find. Identified by a large wooden sign that said BENJAMIN SLOAT, DIRECTOR, it occupied an entire dome supported by concrete pillars at the water's edge. Gail thought the structure looked like one of the Martian ships in the movie version of *War of the Worlds*. Still, she had to admit that the dome was impressive. And it had a wonderful view of the bay. She found the door and went in.

A cadaverous woman of indeterminate age guarded the director's inner sanctum. Tall, gaunt, with iron grey hair twisted in a braid on top of her head, very properly dressed in a crisp white blouse and a navy skirt, she gave Gail a wintry smile.

"Miss Murray, I presume?" she said looking meaningfully at her watch. "We expected you somewhat sooner."

Gail was not intimidated. She had met dozens of these gorgons before. "It's Dr. Murray," she told her firmly. "And I, too, expected to be here somewhat sooner. Unfortunately, Antillean Airlines had other ideas."

"I see," the woman said, her eyebrows lifting. Gail could see her mentally shifting gears, re-evaluating. She decided to try a little amateur psychology.

"You must be Miss Liszt," she said. "I really appreciated your help, especially your prompt replies to my telegrams. Starting a new job is always hard, but it's doubly hard when you have to come halfway around the world to do it."

Miss Liszt touched her hair, evidently thrown a little off-stride by the compliment. She soon recovered. "Rendering assistance to new personnel is part of my job," she said coolly, sounding as though she was quoting from her job description. She glowered at Gail. "And Dr. Sloat was most insistent that your computer file be opened as soon as you had accepted the job. He seems to think you are," she pursed her lips as though the next words hurt her, "indispensible to his cavity project." She looked sternly at Gail. "And the cavity project is very important to Dr. Sloat. Very important indeed. I trust I need not elaborate." She smiled, a ritual baring of teeth that could never be interpreted as friendly.

No, you certainly need not, Gail thought. Now I know exactly where I stand. So I'm indispensible am I, Miss Liszt? And you just hate it. "I understand perfectly," Gail assured her. "If Dr. Sloat is ready to see me . . ."

Miss Liszt smirked in satisfaction. "I'm terribly sorry, but he's not here. When it became evident that you were going to be three hours later than anticipated, well, Dr. Sloat simply had to leave."

"He had to what?" Gail asked incredulously.

"Leave, Miss Murray. Leave. He took the Institute's helicopter to the mainland. He does have other engagements, you know."

"I see," Gail said tersely.

"You should run along and get settled in," Miss Liszt suggested. "And do take the rest of the afternoon to get yourself oriented. There's an information packet in your room. Divemasters meet with Dr. Sloat at six a.m. sharp, so you'll want to get your rest."

Gail briefly considered playing dumb about the divemaster job, but decided against it. Russ hadn't sworn her to secrecy. Presumably it was common Institute knowledge. "Not so fast," Gail told her. "I was never consulted about the job of divemaster. As far as I'm concerned, I'm just a researcher here. And a researcher I'll stay until I talk with Dr. Sloat about it."

Miss Liszt grinned her hyena grin. "You can talk to me about it."

Gail shook her head. "I'd be delighted to do so if your name appeared on my contract. Unfortunately Dr. Sloat signed for ISAUR. He hired me. I believe I'll wait and talk to him."

Miss Liszt blinked a few times. "Very well. But I have to inform you that your dive team will be fined one hundred dollars for every day that you arbitrarily decide not to dive." Her lips twitched in delight. "And it's customary for the divemaster to pay the fine."

Gail gritted her teeth. "When will Dr. Sloat be back?"

Miss Liszt consulted her appointment book. "Let's see . . . today's Tuesday . . . not until Thursday."

"Fine," Gail told her. "I want to see him Thursday. First thing in the morning — before the divers go out. Do you think he'll be free," she asked sarcastically, "or is he likely to have another engagement?"

Miss Liszt raised an eyebrow in disapproval. "He has no other appointments at that time. Shall I pencil you in for, oh let's say five a.m.?"

"Do that," Gail said. "I'll be here."

Miss Liszt closed the appointment book decisively. "Five a.m. Thursday, Miss Murray."

Gail paused on her way out, her hand on the doorknob. "Five a.m. Thursday. And it's Dr. Murray," she told Miss Liszt, turning to look directly at the other woman.

Miss Liszt held Gail's gaze for a moment, then smiled and turned back to her word processor. "Welcome to ISAUR," she said.

Gail slammed the door as she left.

* * * * *

She found Russ washing down some SCUBA gear in a small hut at the end of the dock. He turned off the hose as soon as he saw her.

"I'll just put these tanks back on the rack," he told her. "Today's my day to make sure all our equipment is clean and ready for tomorrow." He laughed a little bitterly. "The dive shop kids should do this, but they've all gotten together and decided there's a jinx on our team, so they won't touch our equipment."

"But that's ridiculous," Gail said.

"Tell me about it," Russ agreed. "Fortunately, Toshio and I know how to fix most things. Brian and Grant — the other half of the team — are, well, good at other things," he said diplomatically. "They're better divers, for instance. Give me just a minute and I'll be done." He lifted the heavy SCUBA tanks back onto their racks, wiped his hands on his shorts, and came back out onto the dock. "I put your gear in your room," he said. "Ready to check out the ISAUR Hilton?"

"Sure," Gail said dispiritedly.

"I see you met our Miss Liszt," Russ observed. "She's enough to spoil anyone's day. But tell me how things went with Sloat."

Gail told him briefly what had happened, and he shook his head. "Yeah, that sounds like Sloat, all right. He spends more time on the mainland than he does at the Institute these days. But that doesn't help you, does it? Now you have to wait until Thursday to straighten things out."

They approached a long two-story white stucco building with a large arched entryway. Russ led her inside. "This is it?" she asked in surprise.

"Home," he said, gesturing her up the stairs.

Gail was impressed. "It's nicer than I expected," she remarked. "Cool, clean, and it even seems quiet. In fact, it reminds me a little of a motel."

"Well, it was part of a hotel," Russ told her. "The Institute's main buildings were once an island hideaway for expatriate Dutch tycoons and mainland landowners. But the place sort of fell into disrepair, and eventually its owner gave it to the Institute's first director."

They passed several rooms and finally came to an open area that contained couches and tables, a television set and stereo, and bookcases crammed with magazines and paperback books. "Our relaxation area," Russ told her. "Beyond this are the women's rooms. The men's are back the way we came."

"Segregation?" Gail asked in amusement.

"No, no, nothing like that," Russ assured her. "But when ISAUR first started hiring women, there were so few of them that they wanted to be together. For moral support I guess. Or maybe to borrow each other's deodorant, like my sisters do," he teased. "So they took these rooms at the end of the top floor. Then, as more and more women came to work here, they just joined the others." He looked at Gail. "But if you want to be someplace else, there are lots of empty rooms. I just thought —"

"This will be fine," Gail said. "Let's see the room."

Russ produced a key and unlocked the door. Her bags had been placed carefully on the room's one bed, and the curtains were open, affording a wonderful view of the ocean.

"I chose a room for you on this side," Russ said. "I thought you'd like an ocean view. Also, the breezes at night are wonderful. Unfortunately it's hot during the day — there's no air conditioning — but the nights are great. And on the top floor you won't have anyone walking on your ceiling. Look here," he said, opening a sliding door onto a little balcony. "See those pines over there?"

Gail followed him onto the balcony and looked toward a clump of trees whose tops were just about at eye level, perhaps ten feet from where they stood. "There's a wild parrot nest in the near tree," he said, whispering. "I saw the parents the other day. If you keep your eye on the nest, I bet you'll soon see baby parrots. This particular species — the Caribbean green-faced paroquet — is on the endangered list," he explained. "You may be one of the last people to see these baby parrots in the wild. It's sad," he said, shaking his head. "Now, what else should I tell you? Hmmm. There's an information packet on your desk there, compliments of our Miss Liszt. Oh yes — here's something you may be interested in." He dug in the pocket of his shorts and gave her a key. "This is for the jeep you came in. Institute vehicles aren't supposed to be used for non-Institute purposes during work hours, but . . ." He shrugged meaningfully. "And this particular jeep has a reputation for stalling, so no one wants it anyway." He grinned. "Toshio has a real touch with engines. He can predict almost to the yard when that baby will die. Of course, when *we* drive it, it purrs like a cat. And we can guarantee it'll behave for you."

Gail laughed. "I get it. Thanks. And I might take you up on your offer to use it. This afternoon and tomorrow will be dead time."

"Help yourself," Russ said. "None of us will have time to go anywhere. We were told to get ready to dive tomorrow. With our new divemaster."

27

"Well, you might as well get ready, but don't count on diving," Gail told him. "I'm not doing anything until I see Sloat."

"Okay," Russ said, shrugging. "We could all use a day lying around eating and sleeping. Voorman was driving us a little too hard." He cocked his head. "What about the fine, though? I'm sure Miss Liszt told you about that."

"She did," Gail told him. "I'll pay it."

He raised his eyebrows. "All right. Well, I'd better get back to work. Do you need me for anything else right now?"

Gail shook her head. "No. I'm going to take a shower, change, have something to eat, and go for a drive."

"You might let one of us know where you're going," Russ said, heading for the door. "In case you have a breakdown, we'll know where to look. We all do that," he explained. "The roads are awful, and the unpaved trails are worse. I'm in room seventeen, downstairs," he told her. "You could just slip a note under my door."

"All right."

Russ smiled and closed the door quietly behind him.

A nice kid. Of course he had been instructed by Benjamin Sloat to see that she was properly introduced to ISAUR, but still, he seemed pleasant and willing. She sighed and turned to examine her room.

About sixteen by fourteen feet, the room really did look like a motel unit, and a modest one at that, with its ersatz oak furniture, pale beige walls, and muted goldtone carpet. Still, everything was clean and in good repair. The drapes, open now to a view of the ocean, were heavy gold brocade, well lined and new. There was a bed against one wall, with a green and gold floral patterned bedspread and a night table and lamp beside it. Facing it was a long desk/dressing table/chest of drawers combination. Above the desk, someone had thoughtfully added bookshelves. The third wall was taken up by a window and the balcony door, and the fourth, where she now stood, with the door to the hall and, to her immediate right, the bathroom. It would do, she decided. She began to unpack her clothes.

When everything was hung and folded, she decided to unpack her diving bags before taking a shower. Might as well find out now if anything had gotten damaged in the trip. She unzipped the blue nylon bag and, seeing the unfamiliar contents, hesitated. What? Turning over the baggage tag, she read: "Marike Osten, Osten's Bay, Bonaire, Dutch West Indies." Well, hell, after all that confusion at the airport, she hadn't even ended up with her own bag. She had Marike's. Damn! She zipped the bag closed. Now she'd have to make a trip up the coast to Osten's Bay and switch bags. She flopped down on the bed, kicking off her shoes in frustration. There was no help for it. But the more she thought of it, the more she had to admit that a drive up the coast, and maybe a snorkel in some secluded cove, wasn't such a bad way to pass the afternoon. And hadn't Marike promised her a tour of Osten's Bay? Gail realized that the thought of seeing Marike again so soon was pleasant. She stood up and pulled off her polo shirt. Suddenly, having to make a drive to Osten's Bay seemed like no hardship at all.

Chapter 3

Gail stopped the jeep at a fork in the road. Signs pointed one way to Kralendjik, Bonaire's capital, another way to Slagbaai National Park, the Flamingo Sanctuary at Goto Meer, and Osten's Bay, and a playful third to New York. A little doubtful of the accuracy of the signs, she consulted a map she found in the glove compartment. Yes, Osten's Bay really was at the north end of the island. She was about to refold the map when a paragraph set in small type in the lower corner of the map caught her eye:

"These maps come to you through the courtesy of the Dutch Antilles Resource Development Corporation, DARDCO, a joint venture between Southpoint Industries, Long Island, New York, and Rincon Resources, Venezuela. DARDCO began operations on September 15, 1980. Through its deepwater superport, capable of handling tankers up to 500,000 dwt, DARDCO facilitates transshipment of Mideast, African, and European oil to the USA. It has a storage capacity of 8.3 million barrels on an island with a stable government in a progressive and cooperative political climate."

Gail folded the map thoughtfully and put it back in the glove compartment. Oil shipments? Through a Bonairean harbor? She frowned. Hadn't she heard that Bonaire had declared its offshore waters and reefs a marine sanctuary? She shook her head. Oil and marine wildlife were simply not compatible. There must be some mistake. She'd ask someone at the Institute.

The road curved toward the shoreline, and soon she became aware that she was driving uncomfortably close to the edge of a sheer drop. The view, however, was wonderful. The shallow water just beyond the beach was palest turquoise, the near inshore reefs a mossy green, and beyond the reef, the sea was the color of cobalt. A sign with KARPATA written on it pointed towards a small observation point, and after only a moment's hesitation, she pulled off the road and parked. A set of stone steps hewn into the side of the cliff led down to a rocky beach. As soon as she saw the stone steps, she knew at once where she was — the dive site known as "the thousand

31

steps," one of the island's most famous underwater locations. She counted the steps — there seemed to be not quite one hundred — but she imagined that to a diver carrying fifty pounds of tank, regulator, fins, buoyancy compensator jacket, wetsuit, weights and gear bag, they would feel like a thousand. Resisting the temptation to climb down the steps and snorkel in the sparkling water, she started the jeep's engine and pulled back onto the coast road.

A short distance past the sign to the flamingo sanctuary at Goto Meer, the road turned sharply, following the coastline, and soon she was driving due north. She frowned. Where was Osten's Bay? She had thought the whole north end of the island was nature preserve. As if in answer to her question, a hand-hewn wooden sign appeared, bearing the message OSTEN'S BAY AQUAVENTURES in large white letters, and underneath, in smaller letters: MEALS AND ACCOMMODATIONS, GUIDED REEF TRIPS, SCUBA EQUIPMENT RENTAL AND REPAIR. She raised her eyebrows. The Ostens, whoever they were, seemed to do everything. She followed the arrow and drove toward the beach.

Tall, droopy-branched pines lined the road, and closer to the water were dozens of palm trees. She knew that neither species of tree grew here naturally — someone had gone to a lot of trouble to plant them. The road ended abruptly in a little gravel parking lot separated from the beach by several immense horizontal logs. The lot, designed to hold about a dozen cars, was perhaps half full. A smart-looking light blue van with OSTEN'S BAY AQUAVENTURES professionally lettered on each door, and an old, recently painted jeep with similar identification indicated that the Ostens were somewhere around. She parked her jeep, took the bag she had brought for Marike, and set out.

Unable to resist the call of the water, she took off her shoes and crossed the white sand down to the beach. There were several beach chairs in the shade just above high tide line, and she put her bag and sneakers on one of them. The water was barely cool — maybe eighty degrees. Perfect snorkeling water. Shading her eyes, she looked around.

The bay itself was crescent-shaped, a slightly lopsided semicircle perhaps two hundred yards across. But if the shape of the beach was slightly imperfect, nothing else about it was. Gail had never seen such white sand. It looked like sugar. She waded into the ocean. The shallow water of the bay was warm, and so clear she could almost count the individual grains of sand. In a moment, she realized she was standing almost precisely in the center of the crescent. To her left was a dock and a rather large wooden structure which she guessed was the SCUBA equipment rental facility. Three boats were tied up at the dock — the usual flattop pontoon boats with twin outboards for SCUBA divers and a sleek white runabout with a rolled-back blue canvas top, the name Osten Two on its stern. She shaded her eyes and looked more closely. It seemed to be a Boston Whaler. A good choice, as Whalers were rumored unsinkable.

Perhaps fifty yards farther along the beach to her left, past the SCUBA dock, was another, smaller dock, and, set back under towering palm trees, a large stone house. This must be where the Ostens lived.

She looked the other way. Where were the guest accommodations? She had to look closely in the shadows under the trees before she saw them: half a dozen wooden cabins with shake roofs, each with its own porch and a view of the bay. A larger wooden structure with a roof and roll-up blinds for walls seemed to be the dining facility, with a dozen rustic tables and twice as many chairs arranged in clusters on a concrete floor. Several long tables stood between the structure's support beams, and Gail guessed that the Ostens must serve food buffet style here several times a day. Just outside was a large barbecue pit. All in all, it seemed an informal and sensible arrangement, and she had to admit a growing sense of admiration for the enterprising Ostens.

But where was everyone? She shrugged. A slender young black man of about eighteen, dressed in a pair of khaki shorts and a clean white T-shirt, whistled to himself as he raked the yard around the cabins. "Excuse me," Gail called. "I want to see Marike Osten. Where would I find her?"

The young man leaned on his rake and pointed lazily to the dock. "Up there. Walk to the end of the dock. She's in the SCUBA shop. You got to go up the dock."

She walked quickly up the steps and onto the dock, her sneakers loud on the uneven planks. Her heart had begun to beat a little faster and she marvelled at her own boldness. Approaching the end of the dock, she saw Marike before the other woman saw her. Blond hair shining in the sun, Marike was seated on a stool behind a long counter running across the front of the SCUBA shop. Evidently she was repairing a regulator, as it lay in pieces on the glass in front of her. Her curly head was bent over her task, and her strong fingers deftly manipulated a small screwdriver. As she finished assembling the piece, she put the screwdriver aside and sat up straight, massaging her shoulders. "Well, hello there," she said.

"Hi," Gail said, embarrassed at having been caught staring. "I hope I'm not disturbing you."

Marike yawned and stood up, stretching her arms over her head. "As it happens, you're not. I'm just finished." She noticed the bag Gail was carrying. "I'm sure glad you brought that," she said. "I remembered after I left the airport that you hadn't told me where you were staying." She smiled a green-eyed cat's smile — subtle, inscrutable, disconcerting.

"Well," Gail said, feeling awkward, "I didn't come all this way just to return the bag. I planned to do a little snorkeling. Or, if you weren't busy, I thought I might take you up on your offer of a tour." She tried her best to keep her remarks light and offhand. She needed to protect herself. She did not want Marike to know how very disappointed she would be if her invitation had been just an idle remark.

Marike looked at her watch. "Well, I won't get this regulator finished today anyhow. I have to order a part for it. So why not? I like to play hooky."

The last thing Gail wanted was to get Marike into trouble. "Who's the boss here?" she asked lightly.

Marike looked at her quizzically. "The boss of what?"

This wasn't going well. "Of this." She gestured around her.

Marike smiled. "You're looking at her."

"You're in charge of all this. The manager?"

"Mmmhmm," Marike said. "I own it, too."

Gail was speechless. Why, this was a million dollar operation. The land alone must be worth a fortune. And all those boats and equipment? Tongue-tied with embarrassment, she cast about frantically for an intelligent reply. Damn! Would she never say the right thing to this woman? Fortunately, she didn't have long to agonize. The shortwave radio on the counter at Marike's elbow squawked into life.

"Osten One to base, Osten One to base. Come in, please."

Marike flipped a switch and brought the handset up to her mouth. "This is base, Osten One. Go ahead."

"Marike, it's Peter," said a small frightened voice. "We've got an emergency. Can you come?"

"Peter?" Marike said. "Where's your father? What kind of an emergency?"

"Dad went down with those two divers. When they were getting ready, I heard them say they'd lose Father underwater and head for the caves north of Isla Lucia. No one's come up. I don't know what to do."

"Damn it to hell!" Marike yelled. "Any extra tanks on board?"

"Just mine."

"All right. Just stay calm and stay on the boat. Do NOT go down after your father, hear? I'll be there in ten minutes."

"All right. Please hurry."

"It's one of my divemasters," Marike said, scribbling a note and taping it to the radio. Brushing past Gail she ran out onto the dock and shouted across the yard: "Thomas! Start up the Whaler and bring it alongside. And hurry!" She came back inside, lips drawn into a grim line, and began hauling tanks down off the racks and checking the air pressure.

"Can I help?" Gail asked.

Marike frowned. "Do you know anything about SCUBA equipment? You can attach regulators to these if you do. They're over there in the corner."

"I'm a qualified instructor," Gail answered, fitting regulators to the tanks. "I can surely do something more useful than this." Her own boldness surprised her.

Marike gave her a searching look. "You heard Peter —
two divers are trapped in a cave. Maybe his father, too.
But I can't ask you to come with me. It's just too
dangerous."

"You don't have to ask. I'm volunteering."

Marike hesitated, then nodded. "Take whatever gear
you need from the racks back there. I'll load the tanks.
And be sure to get an octopus regulator." As Gail went
past her, Marike put a hand on Gail's shoulder. "And a
knife."

Gail swallowed. "All right."

* * * * *

Braced against the movement of the boat, they laid
their SCUBA gear out on the deck as the little Whaler
leaped through the water, Thomas — lean, long-muscled,
and coffee-colored — at the controls. Isla Lucia loomed
suddenly ahead — a round limestone upcropping no more
than twenty yards across, as white as a bleached skull. Off
its northern tip, another Whaler bobbed at anchor. A
small figure in the stern waved frantically.

"Anchor alongside Osten One," Marike told Thomas.
"And get on the radio. We're going to need helicopter
service to the decompression chamber in Curacao."

Thomas nodded. No more than eighteen, he struck
Gail as very competent. "Yes, Marike. And Doctor
Hartog? Shall I call him to meet us?"

"Yes. Good thinking. And Lieutenant Klee, too."
Marike put her arms through the straps on her tank's
backpack and shrugged into it, buckling the belt around
her waist. "Keep those shorts on," she told Gail. "I wish
I'd had enough presence of mind to bring a wetsuit. We'll

be lucky if we don't get cut to ribbons on the coral down there." She shrugged. "Well, it can't be helped. Got that knife?"

Gail pointed to the knife in its black rubber sheath strapped firmly to her calf.

Marike grunted. "Don't hesitate to use it if you have to. I don't want one of those damned kids down there killing you. We'll bring them both up if we can, but if they're too panicked, if we can't do it . . ."

"I know," Gail said quietly. "We'll leave them."

"Right." Marike stepped to the boat's swim platform and knelt. "Hand the spare tanks down to us when we're in the water," she told Thomas. "I'll take two. Gail, you take the other one. Give yours to Wim — he's Peter's father. You'll be able to tell him from the others — he's a small, thin, black man. The other two are big, fat, and fishbelly white," she said in disgust. She pushed her hair back behind her ears, spat in her mask and rinsed it. "Are you all right?" she asked. "Don't come if you aren't. I'll manage."

Gail looked down at the cobalt water and steadied herself against the Whaler's rocking. Her heart thudded in her chest and her mouth felt dry. Thomas flashed her an encouraging smile. Backing out now was impossible — what would Marike think of her? It would have been better not to have volunteered at all. "You can count on me," she said. She finished testing her regulator and rinsed her own mask. "I'm all right."

"Okay. Now listen. Just follow me. The caves are at fifty feet. After you give Wim his new tank, take one of mine from me and follow me in." She tested the light strapped to her arm, and Gail did the same. "There's a short tunnel of about twenty yards, and then a T-junction. Take the righthand fork. The left one dead

38

ends, although you wander around a little before you realize it. The righthand one opens out into a pretty big cave, but the opening is narrow. I expect we'll find that the divers lost their lights and couldn't find their way back to the opening. I'll go in with one tank. You come in after me. Pick one of the divers and let him breathe from the other regulator on your octopus rig while you change his tank. Take him to the cave mouth and go up with him. If he's not too panicked, make a decompression stop at ten feet for as long as you can keep him there. If he gives you any trouble, let him go up by himself. He'll have the bends, but we can decompress him later. Okay?"

Gail nodded.

Marike squeezed her arm. "Let's go." She somersaulted off into the water. Gail followed her.

* * * * *

The cold blue water closed around them and for a moment Gail was unable to breathe. Not now, she told herself. Panic later. Marike needs you. So do the trapped divers. She surfaced, took the tank that Thomas handed her, and submerged again, looking for Marike. She saw her at a depth of about ten feet, swimming toward Osten One. Gail kicked with her fins and swam toward her.

Marike had both her tanks strapped together with a weight belt, trailing them with one arm. She motioned Gail to Osten One's anchor line and pointed down. Gail made the okay sign, and started to descend, pinching her nose and blowing air into her middle ear to equalize the pressure as she went down.

At thirty feet the water changed from turquoise to royal blue. She shivered. It was noticeably colder here. At forty feet, the caves came into view.

39

Stark white and pocked like Swiss cheese, the base of the island was a skeletal arm reaching for the surface of the water. Above was the clenched fist of Isla Lucia. Gail looked in amazement. The island sat on a pillar of eroding limestone hundreds of feet deep and as rotten as a dead tree. What prevented it from collapsing under its own weight? As she swam closer, she saw that the base of the island was riddled with caves — some no more than a few feet across, others not quite large enough for her to swim into. The caves the divers had gone into were unmistakable — they were the only openings that could accommodate a diver.

Gail looked back for Marike, but the other woman was already at her elbow. Through the mask's faceplate, Marike's eyes looked concerned but unafraid, and Gail felt encouraged. Perhaps this wouldn't be so difficult. Marike swam past her to the mouth of the cave and floated there, one hand on the limestone opening, looking inside. She motioned Gail nearer and pointed inside the cave. Gail nodded, and took her light from its straps on her arm, slipping her hand through the cord at its base. She flicked it on and shone it into the cave, noting what a feeble light it made in the darkness.

Gail went first, ducking her head to avoid the sharp limestone, praying that her tank valve wouldn't hang her up on the cave's ceiling. Suddenly a small silver torpedo shot toward her out of the blackness — a lone barracuda barrelling for the cave's opening. She bit down on her regulator to keep from exclaiming in surprise. Small creatures who normally avoided the light scuttled behind rocks and dug themselves into the sand as she swam by. A little bat ray flapped past, so close that one of its graceful wings flicked Gail's arm with a cold, unearthly touch. She shivered.

She was so busy looking for the T-junction that she almost missed Wim. A dark shape in a blue wetsuit, he came hurtling out of the darkness toward her and swam literally into her arms. His brown eyes behind the plexiglass faceplate were terrified, and in a moment, she understood why — he had no tank on his back. Had he given his tank to the trapped divers? He must have been very sure that he could make a free ascent. Or had one of the divers pulled a knife and demanded Wim's tank? He fastened his eyes greedily on her regulator, and she handed it to him, keeping a tight grip on it to establish that it was hers. He took two breaths and handed the regulator back to her; she took two breaths and gave it back to him. The beam from Gail's light bounded eerily off the roof of the tunnel, swinging back and forth to reveal Wim's anxious, frightened face. After a few exchanges of the regulator, Gail could tell he was calming. She shook him by the arm, turning the light on the tank she had dropped to the cave floor. He nodded, and she handed the tank to him, helping him into the backpack and turning on the valve for him. She waited until he was breathing comfortably from the regulator, then pointed up. Wim hesitated, pointing back toward the cave. Gail's heart sank. There was no time for an underwater argument. Fortunately, there was no need.

Marike appeared at that moment, a pale wraith materializing from the darkness. She took Wim by the arm and pointed firmly up. He hesitated for only a moment, then made the okay sign, and turned toward the cave mouth. She handed one of her tanks to Gail, squeezed her arm in encouragement, and led the way down the tunnel toward the cave. One down, Gail said to herself grimly. Two to go.

41

At the mouth of the cave, Marike hesitated, sweeping the interior with her light. She held out a hand to prevent Gail from being carried past her, and Gail noticed for the first time the strong current flowing into the cave. The swim back was going to be tough. She turned her light on the cave's interior, looking for the divers. Marike gripped her arm tightly, and Gail shone her light on the rock formation Marike's light had revealed. From behind it came clouds of bubbles. Gail's heart beat faster in apprehension. Marike turned and made the okay sign. A question. Gail signed back, giving the answer. Marike pointed to herself, and to the left side of the rockfall, then to Gail and to the right side. Gail nodded. Marike swam out into the cave, her light's beam a silver lance piercing the darkness ahead of her. Gail kicked with her fins and swam for the right side of the rockfall.

It was every bit as bad as she had feared. The two divers were engaged in a struggle for one SCUBA tank. Wim's tank, Gail guessed. Their own tanks were still on their backs, their regulators dangling uselessly, no bubbles in evidence. One of the divers had his legs wrapped around the tank and was fending off the other one, taking great gulps of air from the regulator. The other diver was tearing frantically at the regulator, dislodging it periodically, sending clouds of silver bubbles upward to the cave's roof.

As Gail watched, Marike swam up to the diver without the tank and took him by the arm. He turned to face her, and she held a regulator up in front of his face. Grabbing it, he shoved it in his mouth and began to breathe. Gail turned her attention to the other diver.

Swimming over to him, she shook his arm and held up the second regulator of her octopus. He saw her but continued his frenzied gulping from Wim's tank. Gail checked the pressure gauge on the tank he held between his knees and shook her head in dismay — it had less than five hundred pounds of air in it. If he continued gulping air at that rate, it should last him only another few minutes. She held the gauge up in front of his mask and shone her light on it. At first his crazed eyes continued to look into space, then they slowly focussed on the gauge. He blinked, and she saw that he understood at least part of what she was telling him. She backed off a little and shone her light on the tank that dangled from her left hand.

Out of the corner of her eye, she saw Marike's light retreating. A small worm of fear began to gnaw at her self-confidence. What if she couldn't handle this alone? What if this man, crazy with fear, unable to think straight, attacked her? She put the thought out of her mind. Just get the job done, she told herself. Picking up the tank, she swam toward him and held it up. He shook his head, cradling Wim's tank in his arms. Insistently she showed him the spare tank. He shook his head again. Exasperated, she swam behind him and began to change his tank. This man was clearly past the point of reason.

She had just reached for his tank valve when she felt it torn from her grasp. In the darkness, the diver's hands fumbled across her chest and face like a pair of loathsome crabs, gouging, pulling, finally locating her regulator and ripping it from her mouth. Damn it — this man *was* crazy! Furious, and more than a little frightened, she shone the light on him, and saw that he now had both hands on her regulator. Getting it away from him would mean a terrible struggle. Give him the tank if he wants it so bloody much, she told herself. But do it fast.

Unbuckling her belt, she wriggled out of her backpack. As the tank came free, she shone her light on

43

the diver. He reached for the tank, wedged it between his knees, closed his eyes, and sucked greedily on the regulator. Her heart sank. The tank was now less than half full. It wouldn't last him ten minutes. What was she going to do?

Her lungs began to ache. She picked up the spare tank, turned on the valve, and put the regulator in her mouth. Exhaling, she cleared her mouth of water, then inhaled, saying a small prayer of thanks as air flooded into her lungs. This tank had no backpack — she would have to swim holding it in front of her, unless she could think of some way to secure it to her back. She shone her light on the diver, but he was crouched over the tank in some private world where all that mattered was air. Wim's discarded tank glinted on the floor of the cave. She prodded it with one fin. Its belt floated free in the water. She picked up one end. Yes, that would work. Unthreading it from the backpack, she buckled it around her waist, then turned to the diver.

What was she going to do with him? His regulator floated in the water like a dead eel, and she grabbed it, pulling a little. The diver clung resolutely to his tank — a terrified, helpless ball of misery. Angry, Gail tugged again, pulling him toward her through the water. An idea occurred to her — but would it work? It would have to. She would haul him out of the cave like a disobedient dog on a leash.

She pulled. The diver offered no resistance. Pausing to put the spare tank between her legs, she repositioned it, then strapped it to her stomach with Wim's belt. She had already decided she would have to swim on her back, towing this terrified lump of blubber behind her.

They cleared the inner cave mouth without incident, but once into the tunnel, the diver seemed to realize that

44

he was in trouble. She felt a hand grasp hers on the regulator, trying to pry her fingers loose. She held on resolutely and gave a terrific tug, swimming harder. The diver tried to pass her. She kicked out at him. Then she understood what must be happening — he had probably breathed up all his air, and now he wanted hers. In a panic, she looked back over her shoulder. Light! The T-junction was just ahead. Giving one last tug, she pulled him around the corner of the junction and kicked strongly, bringing them both to the tunnel's mouth.

Hauling on the regulator with both hands, she pulled the struggling diver out of the cave and let him go. He floated in the water, as white and ungainly as a dead fish. She saw the panic in his eyes as he looked up at the surface of the water. Oh hell, she decided. You'll never make it, you overfed blimp. Not without my help. She unbuckled Wim's belt and pushed the tank away from her. Taking two final deep breaths from the regulator, she held it out to the diver. He grabbed the regulator with one hand and the tank with the other. As soon as she saw he was breathing, she took him by his leash and swam for the surface. One struggle, damn you, just one, and I leave you here, she thought at him. Either we make it together, or I make it alone. I'm not dying here with you.

The diver gave her no resistance. Perhaps the sight of the surface so tantalizingly close had restored his sanity; perhaps he was simply too weak to struggle further. Decompression stops were out of the question. She would have to bring him up and hope that he could be airlifted to the decompression chamber before he suffered too much. And you, what about you, she asked herself. Exhaling a little, she ascended no faster than her bubbles — a quick way of judging safe ascent speed. I'll be all right, she repeated in a kind of litany. I'll be all right, I'll be all right. She exhaled a little more, kicking slowly, trying to ignore the tightness in her chest, the pounding in her head, the desperate craving for air.

At thirty feet, she knew she wouldn't make it. A high singing sound had begun in her head, and it was difficult to think. She looked down at the diver she was towing to the surface. Nothing made sense. Don't give up now, a voice said in her head. But I can't do it, she whimpered. I'm too tired. I don't know what I'm doing here in this cold water when all I want is to close my eyes and sleep. And I want to breathe. I want to take great gulps of cool air. Why am I holding my breath? Exhausted, she let go her hold on the diver and hung there in the water, confused. Surely she was on the surface — weren't those shapes clouds moving against the silver blue sky? She must be lying on her back on a hillside, watching them. It must be spring — the air was wonderfully cool. She decided to take a breath.

Opening her mouth, she exhaled the last of the air in her lungs. She felt the sun on her face, and, suddenly, noises replaced the singing in her head. She breathed, and cool, fresh air flooded into her lungs. Sobbing, she took breath after breath as consciousness returned. Someone's arms were around her. She opened her eyes. Marike was in the water with her, holding her, supporting her head above the water. Gasping, unable to get enough air, she realized how close to death she had come.

"My God," Marike said, removing Gail's diving mask and emptying it into the sea. "Your mask is full of blood. Thomas — give me some help here!" She raised one of Gail's hands over her head, and someone took it, then her arms, and Gail felt herself lifted out of the water onto the Whaler's swim platform. Someone took off her fins, and she tried to say not to bother, but she had forgotten how

46

to speak. Her mind provided the words, but her mouth refused to function. Blood, she thought fuzzily — what blood? Then she realized why she couldn't think, or speak, or move. My God, she thought, I've got the bends. I'm paralyzed.

Chapter 4

Gail dreamed she was being pounded. But as consciousness slowly returned, she realized that the bone-jarring thumps were being made by a boat as it leaped from wave to wave. But which boat? Where was she? She opened her eyes. She was lying on a worn teak deck, her head on a life jacket. The Whaler. This was Marike's boat. Memory came flooding back, and she closed her eyes tightly, wanting the darkness of oblivion again.

"Give it more gas, damn it!" Gail heard Marike yell at Thomas. "Get us up out of these waves — they're pounding us apart! She'll be awake any minute —

probably in terrible pain. Don't add to her misery!" Gail felt a surge of power from the Whaler's powerful inboard motor. The deck tilted a little as the boat lifted its bow to plane. The thumping was gone; the ride was almost smooth.

She waited for the pain of the bends to hit. In her mind's eye she saw millions of tiny nitrogen bubbles fizzing through her bloodstream, seeking a way out. She remembered her diving instructor illustrating this point — he had shaken up a bottle of Coke, then uncapped it. The spurt had been impressive. And sobering. But unlike the Coke, which had simply gushed out of the bottle, the nitrogen in her body had nowhere to go. The bubbles she had breathed at sixty feet — at a pressure four times as great as surface pressure — were trapped in her body, expanded to four times their original volume. Something had to give. Would they settle in the hollow spaces of her joints, causing the excruciating, crippling pain most common with the bends? Or would one of the bubbles lodge against her optic nerve, rendering her blind? She had seen both happen to careless divers, and neither picture was pretty. She grimaced: careless divers. She had never been careless. It wasn't fair that this was happening to her. Damn that diver anyway! She bit her lip, frightened of what the next few minutes would bring. Sweating, she waited. A few moments passed and, miraculously, nothing happened. She risked opening an eye. Still nothing. Encouraged, she sat up, wiping at the trickle of blood that ran from her nose.

Marike turned, saw her, and left Thomas at the wheel. "Jesus," she said, kneeling beside Gail, green eyes anxious. "Lie down. We'll be there soon. Are you in much pain?"

Gail shook her head again. "No. None."

Marike raised her eyebrows and felt Gail's knees and elbows. "Any pain here?"

Gail shook her head again, hardly believing it herself. "No. Everything seems to be all right. Except for my bleeding nose."

Marike wiped away the blood with a wet towel. "You must have ruptured some of the small blood vessels in your sinuses when you came up so fast. There was a lot of blood in your mask, but the bleeding seems to have stopped." She sat back on her heels, frowning. "Are you having any difficulty hearing? Seeing?"

"No. Nothing seems to be wrong." It was true. How had she escaped the bends?

Marike shook her head. "I don't completely understand it, but I don't think you're going to have the bends. Or an air embolism. I've seen things like this happen before." She shrugged. "You must have emptied your lungs before you reached the surface. And you probably weren't down quite long enough to need to decompress." She took one of Gail's hands in hers and looked at her steadily. "I can't tell you how glad I am you're all right."

Gail returned the pressure of Marike's fingers, for a moment oblivious to everything but those green eyes and he cold hand in Marike's warm ones. "What about the others?" she asked. "The divers. And Wim — how is he?"

"The divers are in bad shape. Serves them right, if you ask me. One of them is already bent. We'll send them both to the decompression chamber just to be sure. I don't know about Wim," Marike said. "He seems to be all right so far, but I'll have to watch him."

Gail looked around. "Where is he?"

"On Osten One. Peter has the wheel. He's keeping an eye on his father, who's keeping an eye on the diver you brought up."

Gail felt a hot fist of fury grip her heart. "He nearly killed us both!" she exploded. "He just kept grabbing tanks."

"I thought something like that might be happening," Marike said grimly. "After I brought my diver up, I started to worry about you. I thought you'd be right behind me. I was just going back down for you when I saw you floating to the surface. I caught you by the hair and pulled your head above water, hoping it wasn't too late." She squeezed Gail's hand.

The Whaler slowed, the bow dropped, and over Thomas' shoulder Gail saw the dock of Osten's Bay come into view. Several men waited there, one running to catch the rope Thomas threw him. Marike leaped from the Whaler's deck to the side of the boat and up onto the dock, ignoring the hand a tall, blond man held out for her.

"Lieutenant Klee," she said, nodding to him curtly.

"Where are they, Marike?" he asked, looking around officiously. His Dutch ancestry, like Marike's, was evident in his tall, strong build, light eyes, and fair hair. Deeply tanned, he looked like a casting director's idea of a Caribbean policeman in his crisp khaki shorts and shirt.

"Just behind us," Marike told him. "In Osten One. They need to go to Curacao to be decompressed. I don't think Wim or this young lady need to go, however."

Klee grunted. "DARDCO's helicopter is waiting up the beach. They didn't hesitate when we asked them." He shrugged. "I suppose you'll leave it to me to thank them."

"You suppose correctly," Marike said, crossing her arms. "I have nothing to thank them for."

51

"They're being extraordinarily generous," he said simply. "I would think that might make you a little better disposed toward them."

The undercurrent of tension between Marike and Lieutenant Klee made Gail uncomfortable.

Marike snorted. "Better disposed toward them? After what they did to my father? Hardly."

Klee sighed patiently. "I know what you think. But there's no proof, Marike. It was an accident. Can't you just forgive and forget?"

A motor roared behind them and Marike turned. "Let's save this discussion for later, Rolf. Right now we have a problem." Peter, a skinny boy of about eleven, with medium brown curly hair and café au lait skin, brought Osten One deftly alongside the dock. Gail was surprised at how little he resembled Wim. Marike caught the rope Peter threw her and tied the boat to the dock. The two divers sat wrapped in blankets in the stern, one with his head in his hands, the other — the one Gail had rescued — holding his elbows and weeping uncontrollably.

A bearded, white-haired man with a black bag whom Gail guessed to be Dr. Hartog hurried up the dock and jumped down into the boat with the divers. Wim stood with his arm around Peter, watching the doctor. "This one for sure," Hartog called up to his assistant. "You'll have to help him to the helicopter." He bent to examine the other diver, the one sitting listlessly with his head in his hands. Hartog stroked his beard and grunted. "Probably him, too. Wim, give us a hand."

Wim supported one diver, Hartog's assistant the other, and they walked down the dock to the beach where the helicopter waited.

"I'd like you to look at Wim, too," Marike told Dr. Hartog. "I'm not sure about him."

Hartog put a fatherly arm around her shoulder. "I'll take a good look at him. Don't worry. But what about you?" He stepped back and peered at her closely. "Those cuts on your legs need a little attention."

Marike shrugged. "Some peroxide and they'll be fine. They're just scrapes."

"All right," Hartog said. "I'll let you know about the divers."

Marike nodded, looking thoughtfully at his retreating back. Then she turned to Rolf Klee who was waiting patiently for her, hands in the pockets of his shorts. Marike walked over to him, and Gail noted what a handsome couple they made.

"I'd like to give you my statement now," Marike told Klee. "I want there to be no doubt about what happened in case those two jackasses decide they want to sue me for negligence. Also," she said indignantly, "I may press charges against them myself. Their diver's certification cards probably belong to their friends. Arrogant bastards. What makes them think that SCUBA diving is as easy as a dip in a hot tub? Damn them anyway! They put Wim's life in danger, as well as mine and Gail's."

Klee nodded soothingly. "All right. Did you get them to sign the usual release forms?"

Marike nodded. "Yes. But I don't want to rely on them. I don't know how well they'll stand up in court. I've never had an accident at Osten's Bay, so I've never had to test them. I might still have some legal liability."

"Possibly," Klee said. "But only if it could be proven that you were negligent. I doubt you were. You're a damned unreasonable woman, but you run a good

53

operation here. I'll take your statements, then go over to Curacao to talk to the divers. I don't think you have anything to worry about." He ran a hand through his short blond hair. "Do you really want to press charges?"

"Maybe," Marike answered, looking at him suspiciously. "Why? Do you think I'm just being a hysterical female? Overreacting?"

Klee closed his eyes wearily. "I didn't say that, Marike."

Marike snorted. "No, but you thought it, didn't you? You're transparent, Rolf. You always have been."

"Damn it, ever since your father disappeared —"

"Leave my father out of this," Marike told him quietly. "I'm running Osten's Bay Aquaventures now, and I'll take care of business as I see fit. And if I want to press charges against those two brainless buccaneers, I will."

Klee shrugged. "Have it your way. You usually do," he added resignedly. "Why don't I go to the shop? You can finish up here, go change clothes, and meet me there."

Marike nodded. "All right. Make yourself comfortable. There's some cold beer in the back by the air compressor. You know where. Give me fifteen minutes or so."

Klee walked slowly away up the dock and Marike shook her head, stepping back down into the boat where Gail waited. "Thick-skulled Dutchman," she said with a certain amount of affection. "He's just like me. Maybe that's why we've never gotten along."

Gail looked at Marike thoughtfully. It was obvious that her new friend was fonder of Rolf Klee than she wanted to admit.

"Let's take a look at your coral cuts," Marike said briskly, changing what was clearly a painful subject. "Then, I insist you be my guest. For dinner at the very least." She shaded her eyes, looking at the sun. "It'll be sunset in an hour or two. Unless you have to get back to your hotel, why don't you stay over?" She smiled at Gail. "Would you like to?"

"I'd like to very much," Gail said honestly.

"It's settled then," Marike told her. "And before dinner we'll try to see the green flash."

"The green flash?" Gail asked, looking at her curiously.

Marike laughed. "A Bonairean specialty. Something like the Northern Lights. When atmospheric conditions are just right, the sun gives off a green flash just as it disappears behind the horizon. Seeing it is supposed to bring good luck."

"Have you ever seen it?" Gail asked.

"No," Marike said. "I watched for it every evening when I came back here after college, but I didn't see it. That was twelve years ago. Then, after my father disappeared, I gave up." She made a face. "I figured waiting for the green flash was about as silly as waiting for luck."

"Oh? Don't you believe in luck?"

Marike frowned a little. "I'm not sure. I haven't been very lucky. Does that mean luck doesn't exist? Maybe not. Maybe it just means I haven't had my turn yet. Or maybe we have to go out and make our own luck in this life." She shrugged. "I like to think I'm still open to the idea that there might be something as mystical as luck. Just as there might be such a thing as the green flash." She gave Gail a dazzling smile. "Who knows — maybe we'll see it tonight. Now, why don't you come on up to the house and I'll fortify us both with a couple of belts of good Dutch gin before we pour peroxide on our cuts."

* * * * *

Gail sat on the porch of Marike's house, a gin and
tonic in hand, waiting for her new friend to finish
showering and join her. Gail had showered while Marike
was at the dive shop talking to Rolf Klee. Now, dressed in
a pair of white shorts and a blue T-shirt belonging to
Marike, she sat in a pleasant glow of fatigue and
inebriation. She was grateful to Marike for suggesting
that she spend the night — she was simply too tired to
navigate the winding coast road back to the Institute.
Clinking the ice cubes in her drink, she smiled ruefully.
No, fatigue wasn't the only reason she was glad to be
staying. If she were honest with herself, she would admit
that the prospect of spending more time with Marike was
appealing.

Why do I want to see more of this woman, she asked
herself. Is it because she, too, is a woman in a man's
world, doing a job similar to mine? Do I want her for a
friend? She considered this possibility. I've never had a
woman friend, she realized. Possibly because I've been
afraid. Afraid of the intimacy. Disturbed by the
realization, she took another sip of her drink.

A door opened behind her, and she heard Marike
talking to her housekeeper Juliana, Wim's wife.
Mouth-watering smells had begun to waft from the
kitchen. Gail guessed that supper must be almost ready.
She stretched, enjoying the unaccustomed luxury of
having no place to go and nothing to do. Of having
someone else make the decisions about what to cook and
when to serve it. Of being waited on. She chuckled. Watch
it, she told herself. You could get used to this.

Marike came out onto the porch, closing the screen
door behind her. She wore a pair of dark green shorts and

56

a pale yellow T-shirt. Her hair was still wet. It clung to her forehead and the back of her neck in little curls. Gail tried not to stare. My God, she's beautiful, she thought.

Marike smiled. "Hi," she said, moving a high-backed rattan chair close to Gail. She put her drink down on the table between them and walked around, lighting the citronella candles sitting in glass globes on the porch floor. "Mosquitos and gnats," she explained. "As soon as the sun sets, they'll be after us. I don't know about you, but I've given enough blood for one day."

Gail laughed. "I couldn't agree more."

Marike raised her glass and clinked it softly against Gail's. "Here's to new friends," she said, her eyes shining.

"To new friends," Gail repeated, feeling her face grow warm under Marike's gaze.

Marike smiled and looked away. "Let's get ready for the flash," she said, putting her drink down. "It's almost time."

Gail joined Marike at the end of the porch. "Come on down here," Marike said, holding out her hand. "The best view is through that clearing between the trees." Marike stood close to her, a hand on her shoulder. "Now watch the horizon."

The sun was a copper ball sliding slowly into the sea, staining the sky peach and lavender, salmon and rose. Gail wondered how she would ever see anything green amid that riot of colors. And would it be bright green, or simply an olive smudge — one color among many? No, Marike had said it would be bright. A flash. Dutifully, she looked. But as the minutes passed, it became more and more difficult to concentrate on anything other than Marike's hand on her shoulder. She does this sort of thing so easily, Gail thought, so . . . naturally. She remembered Marike's hand on her arm as they were about to enter the underwater cave, Marike's fingers pressing hers as they knelt together on the deck of the Whaler. She marvelled. Marike seemed to possess a complete courage — as perfect as Gail's was flawed. Oh, she could swim into underwater caves and rescue divers. She could do that. But such acts were so anonymous. So impersonal. And she was a skilled and experienced enough diver to know how truly low the risks were for her. But to reach out to another human being? She smiled bitterly. She had reached out to Janice two years ago, and the pain of that broken relationship was something she still felt. The enormity of the risks terrified her. She closed her eyes, envying Marike. How do you learn to be like that, she wondered.

Opening her eyes, she noted in dismay that the sun had slipped behind the horizon, leaving only banners of orange and purple to mark its passing. If there had been a green flash tonight, she had certainly missed it.

Marike squeezed Gail's shoulder. "Did you see it?"

"Well, no," Gail said awkwardly.

"Neither did I," Marike said, laughing a little. "But then, I never have. Come on, let's have dinner."

Gail was uncertain whether she was more relieved or disappointed when Marike took her hand from her shoulder.

They sat at a little table in the kitchen and ate swordfish in a marvelous lemony sauce, rice, and a green salad.

"Juliana's going to grill the rest of the fish and feed it to the guests," Marike explained. "Someone caught it deep sea fishing today and brought it back for dinner. We usually don't cook for the guests — most meals are buffet style: cold meat, cheese, bread, tomatoes, fruit. Divers aren't a fussy bunch." She poured Gail more wine, took a sip from her own glass, and yawned. "Excuse me," she said laughing. "It's not the company, I assure you." After a moment, she gave Gail a long look — speculative, charged with meaning. "You know," she said slowly, "though I know nothing at all about you, I feel I know you because we shared a profound experience today. And in a way, I do know you."

Gail looked at Marike across her wineglass. It was uncanny, but those had been her thoughts, too: how little she knew about this woman, and yet how much. "Perhaps you should tell me what you think you know about me," she said cautiously.

"I know you're courageous." Gail flinched a little at this but let it pass. "I know you don't panic under pressure; I know you're resourceful. And I know I'd pick you to have at my back underwater any time. There aren't many people I'd trust with my life," Marike said softly. "And these are things you rarely come to know about someone else. Even your close friends. I've told you I'm not mystical, and I'm not. I'm really very practical. But I think it's significant that we've come to know each other in this way."

Gail looked at Marike helplessly. She longed with all her heart to say what she felt, to tell Marike what was on the tip of her tongue. But her caution would not let her speak. I feel as though you're someone I should have known but never did, she thought. Maybe someone I wanted to meet but never had the chance to. Or the nerve. She swallowed, painfully aware of how clear these thoughts were in her mind. In fact, ever since she had awakened on the deck of the Whaler, she had been amazed at how her thoughts had become sharp and focused. Ideas which had been only half formed were suddenly, simply, complete. She blinked. She had come close to death today, and that seemed to reorder her thinking. But do I want to get involved with you? Memories of Janice were suddenly acute — the misunderstandings, the arguments, the tears, the sleepless nights, the drinking. What do you want with me, Marike Osten?

"I'm glad we've come to know each other, too," Gail equivocated.

Marike yawned again. "I can't keep my eyes open. I'm afraid I'm good for nothing but bed. We'll have to wait until tomorrow to exchange our life stories. And for you to have that tour."

Gail yawned too, suddenly aware of how heavy her arms and legs felt. "That's fine with me. What about these?" she asked, gesturing at the dishes.

"Leave them," Gail said. "Juliana will come back in an hour or so and clean up. Come on. I'll show you to the guest bedroom."

Gail followed Marike down a wide hall to an isolated wing of the house. "In here," Marike said, reaching past her and turning on a light switch. "There are clean sheets on the bed, towels and soap in the bathroom. I get up about six and have a swim. If you're interested, I can wake you."

"I'd like that," Gail said. "Goodnight."

* * * * *

She woke with a start, hearing raised voices somewhere close by. She switched on the bedside light and sat up. It was just after one, her watch told her. The voices grew loud again, and she swung her legs out of bed. Maybe she should go see if Marike was all right. She stepped out into the darkened hallway and paused in the shadows. The voices were coming from the living room.

"— don't think you know what you're doing anymore!" said a loud voice she recognized as that of Rolf Klee. Interesting. What was the police lieutenant doing here at one o'clock in the morning?

"But that's my business, isn't it, Rolf," Marike said with equal heat. "Just because your father was my father's friend you think you have some special rights. Some claim. Well, you haven't."

"Oh, Marike," Klee said in exasperation. "Don't you realize I'm just trying to help? To make things a little easier for you?"

"Easier? I don't need things easier. I need justice. Find those bastards from DARDCO who ran my father down at sea! Wim described their boat for you. What more do you need?"

"Wim's not a very credible eyewitness," Klee said. "You know that."

"Ha!" Marike said. "He can hardly talk straight when you're around because you glare and bluster and intimidate him. He's afraid of you, damn it! But he'd do just fine in front of a jury. No, Rolf, what you really mean is you're afraid to bring charges against DARDCO. You'd be on the carpet in Government House so fast it'd make your head spin. And an hour later you'd be out of a job."

"You're right," Klee said angrily. "I *am* afraid to bring charges against DARDCO on such flimsy evidence. I'd surely lose my job. I'm sorry you find such caution foolhardy. But if you can bring me something solid, some real proof —"

"Oh, leave it alone, Rolf," Marike said. "I'm too tired to talk any more."

"Damn it all, Marike. Why didn't your father sell DARDCO that bloody island of his and have done with it?"

61

"You know why," Marike said wearily. "He wanted to keep the ocean around Bonaire clean a little longer. None of you seem to care about things like oil spills, acid trickling into the sea, the destruction of reef habitats. Well, my father did. And you know as well as I do that's why he died."

"So you say."

"Yes. So I say. And you'll never argue me out of that belief. Go on home now. It's late. I wouldn't have let you in at all, but I was afraid you'd bang the door down."

"Oh?" Rolf asked softly. "Are you sure you didn't let me in for another reason?"

"I won't listen to that sort of thing any more. I warned you," Marike said, her voice cold. "I thought I made myself clear last time. All we can ever be is friends."

"Why?" Klee asked angrily. "I don't understand you. I've loved you since we were kids. And at one time, you loved me, too. We talked about getting married, for God's sake. What would be so terrible about that?"

"Just go, Rolf," Marike told him.

Gail heard Klee make an exasperated noise. "I'll never understand you, Marike. Never!" He was silent for a moment, then he became the crisp professional again. "I'll leave these papers with you. Just sign them and get them back to me later today. I apologize for the rush, but we need to file them before those two divers press *their* charges against you. I'm sorry things are turning out this way. But we're all behind you. I'll keep in touch."

Gail heard the front door close. She retreated into her bedroom and sat on the bed in the darkness, not wanting Marike to see her lurking in the shadows, eavesdropping. She heard Marike go into the bathroom and close the door. Gail yawned, wondering what to make of what she had heard. Marike blamed DARDCO for her father's death at sea, and Rolf for not investigating the incident more thoroughly. Could there be any truth in it? She frowned. Marike didn't strike her as the type to imagine things.

And then there was Rolf's apparently unrequited love for Marike. That was something she certainly wanted to think about later.

The hall light went on as Marike came out of the bathroom. Gail saw her pass the partly closed door of the guest bedroom and hesitate there. She heard Marike's hand on the doorknob, then, slowly, silently, the door swung open. Gail's heart began to thump so loudly she was certain Marike could hear it.

"Gail," Marike called softly, tentatively.

Gail waited a moment, closing her eyes, willing all this away.

"Gail," Marike called again.

"Yes," Gail finally answered.

"You're awake then," Marike said quietly.

"I heard voices."

"Rolf Klee," Marike explained. "He came about an hour ago to drop off some papers for me to sign." She was silent then, and for a moment Gail thought she had gone back to her room. When she spoke again, Gail was surprised at how Marike's voice in the dark pleased her. "Well . . ." Marike said.

"Would you like to come in and talk?" The words were out of her mouth before she realized it.

There was silence for a moment. Then Marike replied: "Aren't you tired?"

"Tired, yes; sleepy, no."

Marike opened the door and came to sit on the edge of the bed. By the light in the hall, Gail could see that she wore only her yellow T-shirt. Gail realized with a start that she, too, had very little on. In fact, she was wearing only the T-shirt Marike had given her. She pulled the sheet a little higher around her thighs.

Marike said nothing for a moment. The light from the hall made a pale halo of her hair, and her eyes shone silver in the dark. Gail could see the outline of her small breasts under her T-shirt, and the rise and fall of her chest as she breathed.

"Gail, I . . ." she said softly. Then it seemed perfectly natural that Marike lean over and kiss her gently on the mouth. Gail felt an electric charge pass between them so powerful it short-circuited her ability to think. She knew she shouldn't be doing this, but try as she might, she couldn't recall why. Marike's lips on hers were driving all other thoughts out of her mind. I don't want to do this, she thought desperately. But the thought had no effect on her actions. Shivering, she closed her eyes. Marike's lips felt like warm velvet, and Gail's arms came up around the other woman's shoulders of their own accord. She held Marike tightly, and when Marike's lips parted, Gail felt her own lips open in return. Marike moaned softly, and put her hands in Gail's hair. The tip of her tongue sought Gail's, gently at first, then with an eloquent forcefulness. Gail met the probing tongue with her own, amazed to find her desires as urgent as Marike's.

Marike's hands caressed Gail's throat, her shoulders, the bare skin of her arms, and when she touched her breasts, Gail too moaned. A hot tide of pleasure built within her, growing with Marike's every touch. Marike slid her hands up under Gail's T-shirt and stroked her breasts. She bent to kiss the nipples. Gail arched, pulling Marike's head closer. Marike rubbed her face across Gail's breasts, kissing her skin with warm, soft lips, taking a nipple between her teeth. Gail gasped with pleasure.

Then Marike laid Gail gently on the bed and drew the sheet away from her body. "How lovely you are," she whispered, stroking Gail's thighs.

Gail closed her eyes, torn between wanting Marike to continue kissing and stroking her but also wanting her to stop. To give her time to breathe. Time to think. What am I doing, Gail asked herself. I don't even know this woman. God, do I want to be made love to so much? This has to stop — I have to stop it.

Her hands on Gail's breasts, Marike had begun to kiss Gail's body with slow, languorous kisses, making her weak with desire. Every kiss brought Marike's mouth closer to Gail's trembling thighs, and the thought of what might come next made Gail feel faint. Stop, stop, she cried to herself, knowing that soon she would have to say it aloud to Marike or it would be too late.

She felt panicked. Trapped. She clenched her fists, torn between Marike's soft, warm breath on her thighs and the voice of reason in her mind.

"Wait," Gail whispered.

Marike looked up. She leaned over Gail and smoothed her hair. "Just tell me what you want."

Gail raised a hand and caressed Marike's face. "I'm sorry. I shouldn't have asked you in." She drew a deep, shuddering breath. "What I really want is for you to go."

Marike was still for a moment. Then, with a sigh, she sat up. "Oh," she said quietly. "All right." She stood up and walked to the door, where she hesitated. "What did I do wrong? I thought you wanted me as much as I wanted you," she said.

Gail closed her eyes, hating her nineteenth century Victorian conscience. "Nothing. You didn't do anything wrong. It's me. I just can't seem to. . ."

"Can't seem to what?" Marike asked, clearly puzzled.

"I can't seem to do things like this as easily as you. I guess I need to know you better before . . . I'm sorry."

"So am I," Marike said. She slipped out of the room and into the hall.

A moment later, Gail heard Marike's bedroom door close. She lay there in the dark, unmoving, then wrapped herself in the sheet and closed her eyes.

Chapter 5

She awoke to bright sunlight streaming through the window. Disoriented, muscles aching, she squinted and sat up groggily, wondering where she was. Memory flooded back — she was at Marike Osten's house. Remembering the night before, she cringed. Where was Marike, she wondered. One look at her diver's watch told her it was almost eight, far too late to join Marike in her swim. She wasn't at all certain she wanted to. How could she face Marike?

She got up and walked to the window. Through the palm trees, she could see the ocean, dark blue under a paler sky, the wind ruffling the sea, the sun striking diamonds from the waves. A small white boat bobbed at anchor about a mile offshore. Marike? Perhaps. She turned away from the window, frowning.

Finding her borrowed shorts, she had just stepped into them when a knock sounded on her door.

"Gail, it's Marike. There's a phone call for you." Marike's voice was cool, flat. "From someone at ISAUR."

"Oh," Gail said, zipping the shorts. "I'll be right there." When she opened the door, Marike was nowhere in sight. She hurried into the living room and picked up the phone.

"Dr. Murray?" a breathless young voice answered. "It's me, Russ. I'm sorry to interrupt your time off, but something's happened that I thought you should know. Sloat's back. He came in early this morning by helicopter. I thought you might want to see him. You know — get your business over with today."

"I certainly would," Gail said. "Thanks for letting me know."

"No problem. See you soon. Say, are you really staying at Osten's Bay?"

"Yes. Why?"

"Brother, you've got more guts than I have. If the Ice Maiden hasn't bitten your head off yet, she must like you a whole lot better than she does the rest of us."

Gail gave a guilty start. "I don't understand what you mean."

"I'll tell you later. Miss Liszt is coming. Have to go now."

"All right. Thanks again." She hung the phone up and, thoughtfully, hands in pockets, walked off in search of Marike. After last night's fiasco, she really did have to say something to her before she left. But where was she?

Gail found her on the front porch, slouched in one of the high-backed rattan chairs, feet propped up on the porch rail, a mug of coffee in her hands.

"Hi," Gail said tentatively.

Marike looked up with an unreadable expression. "An emergency at ISAUR?" she asked.

"No, not exactly. I need to talk to the director. Apparently he's back a day early, so I think I'll leave now in hopes I might catch him."

"Good idea," Marike said, looking out to sea.

"Is something wrong?" Gail asked, feeling foolish. Obviously something was wrong.

"Why didn't you tell me you worked for ISAUR?"

Gail shrugged. "I don't know. We were too busy for me to tell you anything. Besides," she said ruefully, "today was supposed to be the day we exchanged life stories."

"Yes," Marike said, looking at Gail with cool green eyes. "It was, wasn't it?"

"Let's talk about last night, Marike," Gail said softly.

Marike shrugged. "There's nothing to talk about. You weren't interested. That's all there is to it." She put her coffee mug down on the table and stood up. "But where you work — that interests me very much."

"I can see that," Gail replied, perplexed. "But why?"

Marike crossed her arms. "Do you know who pays ISAUR's bills?"

"What do you mean?"

Marike made an impatient gesture. "Come off it, Gail. ISAUR is a front — surely you know that. Oh, they do some genuine scientific work, just enough to allay suspicion. But the real work that goes on there is something quite different."

"Is this a joke?" Gail asked finally.

Marike laughed bitterly. "No, my naive young friend, it's not a joke. And I can see now that the shady Benjamin Sloat has fooled you, too. Well," she said, shaking her head, "you'll soon find out all about ISAUR. But not from me. Oh, no. I'm going to let you discover it all by yourself."

"Why? What's the big secret?"

Marike looked at her for a long moment, and Gail saw an instant of uncertainty. But only an instant. Dismissing it, Marike shrugged. "I just can't believe you're as innocent as you seem. ISAUR would never hire such a babe in the woods. And for all I know, they planted you on me." She snorted. "It's just as well our steamy scene was interrupted last night. Who knows what I might have blurted out in the heat of passion."

Stung, Gail lost her temper. "This is ridiculous! Why can't you just come out and say what you mean?"

Marike's eyes flashed green fire. "Benjamin Sloat, under orders from his masters at DARDCO — the wonderful natural resource company that's going to make us Bonaireans all rich — killed my father." Her eyes filled with tears.

Gail could only stare. "What?" she gasped. The conversation she had overheard last night flooded back. So, Marike thought DARDCO controlled the Institute. She shook her head. It was too farfetched.

"I can see you don't believe any of this. Well, you're in good company. And now," she said, looking at her watch, "I have to go to work. Some of us have to make an honest living." She turned and walked past Gail into the house. "I would appreciate your leaving here as soon as you can manage it; however, I wouldn't send anyone off down the coast road without breakfast. Juliana is in the kitchen." She turned and gave Gail a grim smile. "Even the condemned are entitled to a last meal." Hands in her pockets, she walked down the steps and onto the flagstone path that wound among the trees to the SCUBA dock.

"Wait," Gail called after her.

Marike walked on.

"Wait, damn it!"

But Marike was gone.

* * * * *

Gail's tires spat gravel as she took the corner at the Institute gateway. Still angry with Marike, she pulled into an empty parking space and brought the jeep to a squealing halt. Slamming the door, she marched down the path that led to Benjamin Sloat's office.

To her surprise, Miss Liszt was nowhere to be seen. The door to the director's inner sanctum stood tantalizingly ajar. Summoning her courage, she knocked, and pushed it open. A good-looking, lean, suntanned man with dark hair, a well-groomed beard, and keen brown eyes, sat at the desk, reading. He could be an actor, Gail thought. Or a model. This was Benjamin Sloat?

"Yes?" he said, looking her up and down with a practiced male glance. "I'm afraid you have me at a disadvantage, Miss . . ."

"Dr. Murray," Gail said, walking toward him. "Gail Murray. ISAUR's new research associate."

"My dear young woman!" he exclaimed warmly, bounding from behind the desk, his hands outstretched.

Gail was so surprised she simply stood there. Benjamin Sloat took her hands in both of his, pressed them warmly, and led her to the couch.

"Sit, sit," he said, motioning expansively. "We have so much to talk about."

71

She had little choice. She would have preferred to remain standing, but it seemed out of the question. Annoyed, she sat, sensing the advantage passing to Benjamin Sloat. It was clear he intended to control this meeting, and from the little Gail had seen of him she guessed he was practiced in such matters.

"I gather you've already met our Miss Liszt," he said with an apologetic smile. "She's a bit overzealous, I'm afraid. A good worker, but . . ." He shrugged meaningfully. "And of course, she wouldn't have reacted well to you," he said softly, stroking his beard.

"Oh? Why not?" Gail demanded, although she was certain she knew the answer.

"She smells competition, my dear." He cast an appreciative glance at Gail's bare legs. "Serious competition, I might add."

Gail forced herself to stare at him coldly. This was the place in Benjamin Sloat's script where she was supposed to titter and blush or, at the very least, simper a little. Well, he could forget that. I know you, Benjamin Sloat, she thought. I've seen dozens of you. I've even heard you articulate your theory of how to get along with the sexes: deal with a woman from the neck down, and a man from the neck up. You think a few sexually loaded remarks will turn us to jelly. What arrogance! Oh, you've had a lot of success batting those big brown eyes, but thank God I'm immune.

"Tell me about this divemaster business," Gail said, trying to ignore his eyes on her breasts.

He blinked and raised his eyes to hers. "What?" he asked.

For God's sake, Gail fumed silently, I didn't ask you to articulate the Second Law of Thermodynamics — it's a straightforward question. "It seems that everyone but me knows I'm to be divemaster," she said, forcing an even tone.

"My dear," Benjamin Sloat said, laying a soothing hand on her arm. "I would have asked you, believe me, but it all came up so suddenly. And then you were en route." He shrugged. "Besides," he said, lowering his voice confidentially, "there really was no one else. So I thought you would prefer doing the job yourself to waiting until we'd found a suitable divemaster." He stroked her arm a little, riveting her with that intense dark gaze. "Really, you have excellent . . . credentials. So many talents."

She was having difficulty concentrating on Sloat's words, so great was her desire to punch him in the mouth. "I see," she said, removing his hand from her arm. "If I want to get on with my research, and my job, I'll agree to be divemaster."

Sloat shrugged, smiling a little. "Rather bluntly put, but essentially correct."

"All right," Gail said through clenched teeth. "I agree. Reluctantly. Will my salary be adjusted accordingly?"

"Of course, of course," Sloat said.

"When do we dive?"

"Tomorrow morning," Sloat said, suddenly businesslike. "You can see Russ — the young man I sent to the airport for you. He'll see that you get all the equipment you need. Divemasters meet with me at six o'clock — just before you go out. I assign the dive sites then."

"I was wondering about that," Gail said, choosing her words carefully. "Russ told me that you now have a computer program that assists you in selecting likely dive sites. Is this true?"

"Well, yes, in a manner of speaking," Sloat equivocated, clearly uncomfortable.

"I'd like to take a look at it if I could," Gail said. "That is my area of expertise, after all."

"Er, yes, I'm sure you'd like to take a look at it," Sloat replied. "Unfortunately, you can't."

"I can't?" Gail asked in amazement. "Why on earth not?"

"It's proprietary."

"I don't understand."

"The program doesn't belong to ISAUR," Sloat explained. "It's a very recent acquisition. And it wasn't developed by anyone here."

"Who developed it?"

Sloat's brown eyes stared into hers. "An industrial programmer," he said.

Gail was incredulous. "Really?" she asked. "I knew there was a handful of other scientists working in the area of cavity research, but I wasn't aware anyone in industry was working on a project like mine. If there were someone, surely I'd have known about it." This is crazy, she thought. There's just no one else working in this area with the competence to design such a program. And what about her job here? She'd been hired to help ISAUR develop its program. Hell — did she even have a job anymore? Sloat didn't need her. What was she doing here?

"The program's developer isn't anyone you would have known about," Sloat replied soothingly. "A private corporation owns the program."

"Well?" Gail asked.

"Well what?" Sloat replied, sighing, clearly annoyed by her persistence.

"Well, which corporation developed it?" Gail demanded, unable to be polite any longer.

74

"I'm not at liberty to tell you," Sloat answered coolly. "And please, Dr. Murray, calm yourself. I know this is quite a blow for you — discovering that years of work have been in vain. That the real discovery was made by another." He patted her arm again. "You have my sympathies. But that's how research goes, after all. Someone has to make the breakthrough. It's like a race, isn't it? There can be only one winner."

She shook his hand off angrily. "I don't believe it," she told him bitterly. "All that work. For nothing?"

"Now, now," he said soothingly. "Hardly for nothing. Why, just yesterday I was talking with the program's developer. He was describing a few little glitches he had encountered in making the program fully operational, and I mentioned to him that you would soon be with us."

Gail stared at Sloat stonily. "And?"

"And he said he'd be happy to have you work with him as a consultant. He did say that if you were able to iron out the problems in the program, he'd consider giving you credit as co-developer."

Gail looked at Sloat suspiciously. "Oh?"

"Oh yes, my dear," Sloat said, stroking his beard. "This is business, Dr. Murray, not academia. This particular individual has nothing to gain by hogging all the glory for himself. He makes quite a handsome salary as it is. No, he would be quite willing to share the limelight with you. Think of it as the equivalent of co-author status."

So there might still be a way to salvage her life's work. She tried not to appear too eager. "Let me think about it," she said. "In the meantime, what would he want me to do?"

"Oh, nothing much right now," Sloat said. "He'll be getting in touch with you to review the program.

Incidentally, have you downloaded your data into ISAUR's data banks?"

Gail shook her head. "No. I didn't have a chance to do that before I left."

Sloat shrugged. "No problem. Miss Liszt can do it." He handed her a tablet of paper and a pencil. "Why don't you just write down your data file codes. We'll take care of it."

"It's not that easy," Gail said. "Erindale's system is somewhat antiquated, I'm afraid. There are three different levels of coding. I gave Miss Liszt the main computer code so she could take a look at the size of my files, but I really need to download the data files myself."

"All right," Sloat said offhandedly. "But the sooner you do it, the sooner my programmer friend can take a look at what you have and ascertain how the two programs can be meshed."

"Well, all right," Gail said uncertainly.

Sloat looked at his watch and, standing up, began to herd her toward the office door. She realized she had been dismissed. Opening her mouth to protest — she did have a few additional questions — she found her words muffled by the angry drone of a helicopter so close overhead she ducked.

"Where did it land?" she asked in amazement. "On the roof?"

Sloat raised his eyebrows in disapproval of her levity. "Hardly. It landed at our heliport."

"Oh yes," Gail said. "I remember. Russ told me DARDCO donated the heliport, and the helicopter." She thought for a moment, wondering if she should go on. "DARDCO seems exceptionally generous to ISAUR. Getting corporations to fund scientific research is usually very difficult — our priorities are often in conflict."

Sloat had paused, hand on the door. He was looking at her strangely. "Often, but not always," he said with a peculiar expression. "If the parties involved have good will, it's possible to cooperate. Especially if everyone is working toward a common goal."

Gail frowned, puzzled. "Are you talking about ISAUR and DARDCO, or about science and industry in general?"

"I was talking in generalities, of course," Sloat said quickly. "But it has occurred to me that ISAUR might lend DARDCO a hand from time to time. DARDCO has, after all, been exceedingly generous to us."

"Oh? What did you have in mind?" Gail asked.

Sloat hesitated. "What do you know about the international oil situation?" he asked.

Gail was taken aback. "Only what everyone knows, I suppose. That the West now has an oil surplus but the Middle East countries, and OPEC, really control production and prices." She shrugged. "That's about all."

"That's enough," Sloat told her. "You have quite correctly identified the problem, my dear. The Middle East holds all the cards in this petroleum poker game. And the West may wake up too late to discover that its precious surplus has gone. Disappeared. Vanished. The U.S. hasn't sunk a major new well in ages, let alone discovered any new fields. Did you know that the U.S. oil industry halves its commitment to exploration every year?"

Gail shook her head. The only time she thought about oil was when she filled her gas tank.

"The situation is critical," Sloat said. "Unless we find new reserves, we'll be at OPEC's mercy when our surplus is exhausted. Right now, seventy-five percent of U.S. rigs stand idle. The reason? It costs too much to operate them.

It costs OPEC one dollar to bring a barrel of oil out of the ground. Do you have any idea how much it costs us?"

"I'm afraid I don't." Gail stifled a yawn, wanting to disengage from this garrulous man as soon as possible. Like most men, he showed no hesitation in inflicting his preoccupations on his female listeners.

"Seventeen dollars," Sloat exclaimed. "Seventeen! Shocking, isn't it? But if we could lower the cost, why then we'd be energy self-sufficient. We wouldn't need the Middle East." His eyes gleamed. "Think of it, my dear. The whole global balance of power would shift back to the West. To the U.S., where it belongs. And we could shift it."

"We could?" Gail asked politely. "How?"

"By making the oil industry competitive again," Sloat said, looking at her as if she were an idiot. "By cutting costs. By making it possible for every well sunk to hit paydirt. That's how."

"But I thought drilling for oil was a real gamble," Gail protested. "Some of my geologist friends say the odds are like blackjack in Las Vegas."

"They're right," Sloat told her. "Quite right. But if we and DARDCO were to put our heads together —"

"Excuse me," a cool voice called from just beyond the doorway. Gail turned to see the disapproving features of Miss Liszt. "You have a call from Miss Soto on line one," she told Sloat.

"Miss Soto," Sloat said, as if he had never heard the name before. He blinked, and Gail could almost hear him change mental gears. "Oh yes, of course. Tell her I'll be right with her." He turned back to Gail. "We'll have to continue this discussion another time," he said, looking at her strangely. "I have the feeling we may well have similar attitudes on this subject."

"All right," Gail said, wondering what on earth Sloat was talking about. Politics, the Middle East, and the global balance of power couldn't have concerned her less at the moment. How had she inadvertently communicated interest? Or perhaps Sloat was inviting her to view his etchings. Thanks, but no thanks.

"Well then, I'll see you tomorrow morning at six with the other divemasters, Dr. Murray."

"I'll be there," Gail said.

He raised an eyebrow at her lack of enthusiasm. "And you'll get your data downloaded into ISAUR's computer?"

She nodded.

"Good girl!" he said enthusiastically.

She felt herself seething all over again. He was an incredibly aggravating man. "I'll leave you to your phone call," she said, excusing herself. She felt Miss Liszt's eyes boring into her back as she walked through the outer office, and she found herself taking an inordinate satisfaction in pretending the other woman did not exist.

Chapter 6

Gail stood on the path outside the dome, hands in her pockets, feeling depressed and anxious. She looked through the palms at the ocean sparkling in the sun and tried her best to believe that things weren't as bad as they seemed. After all, having your research project pulled out from under you wasn't the end of the world, was it? Maybe it was. Of her world, anyway. What was she supposed to do now — spend the rest of her year at ISAUR as divemaster? She really didn't know. Sloat hadn't been very informative. Shrugging, she walked despondently down the path that led to the dock.

She hardly knew what to make of Benjamin Sloat. On the surface he seemed to be a typical Lothario — roving eyes, wandering hands, easy flattery. But underneath, Gail sensed there lurked something else. Something dangerous. His digression into the politics of oil had been so unexpected, his opinions so passionate and so irrelevant to their conversation. She wondered if all her dealings with Sloat would be five minutes of pro forma ogling, two minutes of relevant business, and fifteen minutes of professorial lecturing.

"Hi, Dr. Murray!" someone called.

She turned to see Russ hurrying up the dock. With him was a small, muscular Japanese youth she assumed was Toshio, his diving buddy. She had to smile. They were an odd pair: Russ tall and thin, Toshio small and compact; Russ pink and sunburned, Toshio brown and tanned; Russ sunny and smiling, Toshio dour and frowning. Mutt and Jeff. She waved. "Hi," she called.

"So how did it go with Sloat?" Russ asked.

She shrugged, reluctant to tell him the whole story. Besides, confiding in him would be inappropriate. He was a student, and, starting tomorrow, he would be someone for whom she would be responsible. "How did it go?" she repeated. "About the way Sloat wanted it to." She told him the essentials. "Meet your new divemaster."

Russ tried to look disappointed. Toshio, however, had not trouble looking even sadder than before. "I'm sorry for you, but not for us," Russ said. "Oh, Dr. Murray, this is Toshio Jin." Russ clapped Toshio on the back.

"How do you do?" Toshio said formally, extending his hand.

Charmed by such manners, Gail shook his hand. "Are you another of ISAUR's students?"

"Students cum research assistants, yes," Toshio told her, scowling. "I'm incarcerated here for a year. My advisor at UCLA thought this would be an enriching experience."

"And it hasn't been?" Gail smothered a smile at Toshio's gloom.

"Not so far," he informed her. "All I've done in six months is take still photographs of various sections of the reef out there." He shrugged, dropping his shoulders under the weight of the world. "Most disappointing."

Russ nodded agreement. "Yeah, that's true enough. The rest of us set up the grid — Toshio has the cushy job." He elbowed Toshio playfully. "But in the past few months, things have been a little different."

"Oh?" Gail asked, alert with interest.

"Yeah. Sloat gives our divemaster the coordinates for several sections of reef, and we test the coordinates for cavities. We've never done that before." He shrugged. "Must be the new computer program. Right, Toshio?"

Toshio snorted. "No. I still maintain Dr. Sloat uses the dart board technique."

"You've been doing this for several months?" Gail asked.

Russ nodded. "Well, two anyway."

Gail frowned. If the Institute had been using its own computer-generated cavity locating program for two months, then why was she here at all? Well, Sloat could hardly have wriggled out of his contract with her — they had both signed it over six months ago. But her last communication with Miss Liszt had been almost exactly two months ago. Something stirred in her memory, nagged at the back of her mind, but for the moment she let it go.

"How do you test for cavities?" she asked.

"Usually we use an air gun to penetrate the reef, and then we stick probes in once we have the holes drilled," Russ told her.

Gail raised an eyebrow. "What do you mean, *usually?*"

Russ and Toshio looked guiltily at each other. "Sometimes our divemaster had us set charges," Russ said.

"Charges? You don't mean dynamite!"

Russ shrugged. "I guess that's what it was." He held up his hands, seeing Gail's expression. "I know, I know," he said. "We could blow our eardrums in. But believe me, it wasn't our idea. All the teams are in such competition for the bonus they'd cut each other's throats."

"Not all of us like this, Dr. Murray. Apart from the danger to us, think of the destruction to the reef," Toshio said mournfully. "After Sloat gets finished running his experiments out there, the reef will be dead. The most complicated ecosystem in the world, destroyed," he said, shaking his head sadly. "The man is a barbarian."

"The man is a maniac," Gail said heatedly. "Well, there'll be none of that while I'm divemaster. We'll leave our eardrums, and the reef, intact."

"I'm all for that," Russ said. "Listen, do you want to pick out some gear now, or would you rather wait until tomorrow?"

"I really don't feel like doing it now," Gail said wearily. "I thought I might have some lunch and then get some sleep."

"Leave it all to us," Toshio said gallantly. "Just tell us what you need and we'll take care of it. A tank, I presume. And what else?"

Gail thought. "Maybe a weight belt. I have my own regulator, buoyancy compensator vest, and fins. So I guess I don't need anything else."

"If you leave your regulator outside the door of your room, I'll check it out," Russ offered. "Sometimes airplane flights don't agree with the diaphragm."

"That's true," Gail said. "Thanks. Well, I guess I'll see you two later." A thought occurred to her. "Say, where is this terrific computer of ISAUR's? And how do I get access to it?"

Russ pointed back the way Gail had come. "It's in the communications dome. That's the small one just beside Sloat's office. And watch out — Marvin the computer operator is a male version of Miss Liszt. He thinks the computer belongs to him in the same way she thinks Sloat belongs to her." He shook his head. "What a pair."

"God, is everything this hard around here?" Gail burst out.

"Unfortunately, yes," Toshio said. "We're quite aware that we are nothing more than slave labor. And extraordinary precautions are taken to keep us common laborers away from any sensitive areas. It would be shocking were we to learn something," he said, deadpan.

"It's like someone has something to hide," Russ said. He thought for a moment, then shrugged. "Say," he said to Gail, brightening, "how did you end up at Osten's Bay?"

"Where?" Gail asked, only half listening.

"Osten's Bay. You know, Marike Osten's place. The Ice Maiden."

"Oh," Gail said weakly. "She's an acquaintance. She invited me for . . . a tour."

"Well, she must be making an exception in your case," Russ said, thoughtfully. "She sure hates the rest of us."

84

Gail nodded. She had no wish to talk about Marike, certainly not with Russ.

Russ and Toshio walked down the dock to the SCUBA shed, and Gail turned and walked up the beach, intending to go to the communications dome. But part way there, she found a cluster of abandoned beach chairs in the shade of a clump of palms. Suddenly tired, she sat down. Putting her head back, she closed her eyes. Just for a minute, she promised herself. She had a brief longing for the cool nighttime breeze on Marike's porch. If things had turned out differently, she could be driving to Osten's Bay where she and Marike would sit on the porch while Gail told her about these unsettling developments. Marike would put an arm around her shoulders and kiss her cheek. Stop it, she told herself angrily. You're a fool. She closed her eyes, resolutely shutting out the sight of the ocean framed by palm trees — a view that now reminded her of Osten's Bay. And although she tried to empty her mind of the divemaster job, her ruined research career, the terrible scene with Marike, she was unable to banish thoughts of the night before.

If she hadn't sent Marike away from her bed, would things now be different? They would have spent all night in each other's arms, with time to talk, time to begin to get to know each other. She clenched her eyelids on hot tears. Why am I such a Victorian prude? she asked herself angrily. I *am* attracted to Marike, I admit it. And spending the night with her would have been extremely pleasant. God knows what happened was pleasant enough. So why couldn't I simply have enjoyed what was offered? Why wasn't that good enough?

She wiped her eyes with the back of her hand and forced herself to look at the ocean. This was a view she would be seeing every day for a year. Perhaps she could desensitize herself to memories of Marike by forcing herself to look at it. But she knew, even as she looked at the blue water, that what had happened between her and Marike was unfinished. A magnetic attraction had drawn them together despite her reserve. Words said in haste and anger could not negate its force. Somehow, the events of last night needed to be dealt with. But how a meeting between them could now come about, she couldn't imagine. What had passed between them was as significant and powerful as the events underwater. And she knew that Marike, too, considered their meeting something more than a chance encounter. Damn it, she thought despairingly, I didn't say I didn't want you, Marike Osten. I only wanted you to give me some time.

She looked at her watch. Just after one. Should she try to sleep? The heat of the afternoon was not conducive to rest. Maybe she'd go for a swim. To hell with Sloat and his demands. She sighed. No, she couldn't do that. She had told Sloat she'd download her research data onto the Institute's computer. She'd better do it.

* * * * *

Gail was barely able to control her temper. This was the third time she had had to run the log-on sequence. What was the matter with Erindale's computer? Or did the problem lie with ISAUR's? She knew she would never be able to convince ISAUR's communications technician that something might be awry with his million dollar baby, so she decided to persist. She looked over the top of her CRT screen at Marvin the technician, a pale, portly, uncommunicative little man who had taken one look and decided to ignore her. Toshio had been wrong: Marvin wasn't cold, he was frozen. She was on her own.

Again Gail logged onto Erindale's computer and received the same initially promising message: "Host is on-line. Enter password." Again she began the tedious process of entering the three levels of passwords. The first two passwords were accepted with no problem, but at the third — the code that would give her access to both her data files and the shorter cavity location program itself — the computer balked.

"Unable to download CavSearch," it told her again.

Exasperated, she sat back. What could be wrong? The last time she had worked on the program — just a week ago — there had been no problem. She decided to open the file and take a look. "Open CavSearch," she typed.

"Unable to open CavSearch," the computer told her. "Error number 701-C present."

"Ridiculous!" she yelled. "What the hell is a 701-C error anyhow?"

"A 701-C error is unauthorized entry," Marvin told her in a condescending tone. "Someone has been mucking around with your files, dearie. They've locked up, I'm afraid."

Gail sat back, flabbergasted. Who could have been trespassing in her files? She shook her head. The whole thing was absurd. Frowning in concentration, she tried to remember the keystroke sequence to override a file lock. After a few false tries, she got it right, and the computer announced: "Ready to download CavSearch." One finger poised above the Execute key, Gail hesitated. She didn't like this. If someone had been looking at her program, who knew what damage had been done. No, she'd better wait to download until she'd had a chance to examine it. In the meantime, however, she'd discourage prying eyes. She created another file, named it "Research Expenses," and copied the CavSearch program development file to it.

She briefly debated the wisdom of wiping the original file, but decided against it. Instead, she opened the CavSearch program and typed a hidden password, and a nasty little surprise, into the opening sequences. Now anyone else who used the program would get an unpleasant welcome. She gave the computer instructions to download her research data onto ISAUR's computer, and sat back, thinking.

Who could be so interested in taking a look at her program that he would have broken into her files? It had to be someone back at Erindale, she reasoned, because he needed the Erindale computer code. And it would be useful if he also had her department's password and an account number to which to charge the computer time, although that wasn't strictly necessary. So, who? Charlie Henderson, the little marine biologist with the perpetually fashionable coiffure? She couldn't imagine him ever SCUBA diving — he would have to get his hair wet. And he was the only researcher at Erindale who had expressed a smidgen of interest in what she was doing. She had always felt her research was safe from him because of his misogynistic nature — he would sooner perish than admit that a woman might know more about the contents of coral reef cavities than he did. How — or when — Charlie ever did any research escaped her. She sighed. Perhaps she had underestimated Charlie. Perhaps he had found a way to make an end run around the necessity for all this tedious research: burgle her files. She shook her head. Just what he intended to do with her program, she couldn't imagine. Well, Charlie was in for a surprise.

The computer finished downloading her research data — detailed accounts of reef ecologies, her attempts to use this information to locate cavities, her successes and failures — and she disengaged from Erindale's computer.

"I'm done," she told Marvin. "The line's free if you want to use it."

He grunted, never looking up from his console.

She shook her head, deciding not to favor him with one of a half dozen sarcastic replies that sprang to mind. Be nice, she told herself. Maybe his life is as depressing as yours is fast becoming. Dejected, she opened the door of the dome and stepped out into the late afternoon light. No, she told herself fiercely, I won't wallow in self-pity. I'll go find a bunch of my colleagues at the cafeteria and force myself to be sociable. Eat, drink, and be merry. For a few hours, I'll file all these worries. Like Scarlet O'Hara, I'll worry about all this tomorrow.

Chapter 7

In the still twilight that precedes sunrise, Gail walked down the path to Sloat's office, shivering a little. She had pulled on a long sleeve T-shirt over her old blue Speedo, and still she felt cold. Well, the sun would soon be up.

Inside the dome, four young men in various poses of resigned impatience sat on straight-backed hairs in front of Miss Liszt's desk. One chair was vacant — Gail presumed it was for her — and she sat down next to a burly young blond in a red bathing suit and a short sleeve pink T-shirt that said PARTY ANIMAL.

"Hi," she said. "I'm Gail Murray."

The blond looked down at her from his lofty height and smiled. "Yeah, we know," he told her. "Jinx Team's divemaster." One of the other divemasters snickered, and Gail felt herself growing angry. So that was how things were going to be. She bit back a few choice words and forced herself to be calm.

The supercilious Miss Liszt appeared from Sloat's office, computer printouts in hand, and favored Gail with a raised eyebrow. "Ah, so you deigned to join us after all," she said, managing to imply not only that Gail was late, but that she was less than enthusiastic about her new duties.

Gail looked guiltily at her watch: five fifty-nine. She wasn't late at all. Aggrieved, she traded glares with Miss Liszt, and crossed her arms over her chest.

"Alec," Miss Liszt said, handing the blond diver next to Gail a sheet of instructions.

He took one look at it, whistled, and folded it in half.

Miss Liszt handed all the men their sheets before handing Gail hers.

"All right, gentlemen," she said, ignoring Gail. "Go to it. And don't forget — your reports are due on my desk by four sharp!"

The four men rose like first graders dismissed by their teacher, and filed out past Gail. She heard them talking on the path outside the dome as they hurried down to the dock.

Finally Miss Liszt noticed that Gail was still sitting there. "Do you have a problem, Miss Murray?"

"Yes," Gail said holding up the sheet she had been given. "I haven't the faintest idea what these coordinates mean."

"Oh dear," Miss Liszt said, shaking a finger admonishingly at her, "it seems as though we haven't read our *Reef Coordinates Guide* yet. Mmmm?"

Gail counted to ten. "We would certainly have read our *Reef Coordinates Guide* if we had ever seen such a thing."

"Now, now," Miss Liszt cautioned. "Sarcasm is hardly necessary. The guide was in the information packet prepared for you. I put it there myself." She peered at Gail over the tops of her glasses.

Gail shook her head. "No. It wasn't."

Miss Liszt flared her nostrils. "Are you calling me —"

"I'm not calling you anything," Gail interrupted. "Just let me have a copy of the bloody guide, will you?"

Miss Liszt clamped her lips together. Taking a bulky softcover book down from a shelf, she handed it over. "I'm noting in your file that you've received two copies of this," she said. "They cost a great deal of money."

"So bill me," Gail said over her shoulder on the way out, hating herself for this petty display of pique but unable to control it.

* * * * *

Russ idled the boat's engine and Brian Elridge and Grant North — marine botany students and the other half of Jinx Team — heaved the anchor overboard. Russ backed the boat up a little to set the anchor, then cut the engine.

Waves slapped at the sides of the boat as it rocked a little in the chop. Gail picked up the plastic writing slate she had brought along and called the students together in the boat's bow.

"We're over a little reef shaped like a battleship," she told them. "In fact, it's called Battleship Reef. The computer has suggested that we look there for cavities, in particular sections 9, 21, 35, and 67." She sketched the reef and the relevant sections quickly on the clipboard. "Any questions?"

They shook their heads.

"Toshio, did you bring the section grid?"

"Yes," Toshio said. "It's in the stern."

"All right, why don't you and Russ go on down and lay out the grid. Brian and Grant can bring the air hammer. I'll carry the probe."

The boys nodded.

"We'll do it this way — when the grid is set, Toshio and Russ will flag the sections. Brian and Grant will hit number nine with the air hammer and then back off. I'll go in and look, and if we have a cavity, I'll drive a pennant piton into the hole. Then we'll tackle the next section."

"Who's going to take the extra tanks down?" Grant asked.

Gail frowned. "What extra tanks?"

"We'll need to change tanks between sections 21 and 25," Grant said.

"I know," Gail told him. "We'll come up and do it."

"Oh," he said.

"Our last divemaster had us change tanks underwater," Russ explained. "He said it saved time."

"Yes, but it increases your bottom time," Gail said. "It's a needless risk. We'll be at seventy-five feet. If you had an emergency and had to come up fast, you'd have the bends for sure. No, we'll play it safe."

"It's fine with me," Grant said. "Just asking."

"Okay then," Gail said, looking around. "Everyone knows his job. Let's do it."

Toshio hit the water first. Russ handed him the bulky yellow nylon rope grid and jumped in beside him. They adjusted regulators and masks, then with a flip of their fins they were gone. Gail left Brian and Grant to their job. She fitted her SCUBA tank to the buoyancy compensator vest, attached her regulator, turned on the tank to test the regulator, and put it aside. Brian and Grant jumped overboard, and she handed them the bulky air hammer. In an instant they too had vanished beneath the surface of the sea. She rinsed her mask, put on her fins, and wriggled into her SCUBA backpack. Backing to the boat's bow, one hand on her mask, one hand behind her to keep the tank from hitting her in the back of the head, she jumped.

The blue water closed over her head, so cold it made her gasp. She knew she would be surrounded by a cloud of her own bubbles for the next few moments, so she methodically went through her checklist: regulator working, mask clear, straps tight, gauges operational, watch functioning. Everything seemed all right. She looked up at the surface two or three feet above her, then down at the bottom, nearly seventy-five feet below. All she could see of Battleship Reef was a blurred suggestion of greenish white. Of the boys, she saw nothing. She swam over to the boat's anchor line, and, one hand on the line, one hand on the air release valve of her buoyancy compensator jacket, she began to descend.

She was struck again, as she was at the beginning of every dive, by the eerie beauty of the world beneath the sea. From the dive boat the ocean looked as flat and empty as a blue plate — a wasteland. Yet just beneath the surface, a whole alien world existed. No one need travel to new planets to find unexplored worlds — here was one on earth.

At forty feet, she encountered the huge Gothic shapes of pillar coral and was forced to swim away from the anchor line to find a clear space among them through which to descend. And although the coral pillars looked soft and velvety, she knew from experience that each rounded pillar was as hard as concrete. Coral was not a rock, or even a plant, but an animal. Coral reefs were alive, each composed of billions of tiny animals — polyps, actually — with slitlike mouth-openings surrounded by tentacles for stinging and trapping food. Cells on the lower sides and bottom of the coral polyps produced the limestone that built islands and reefs. Some reefs were extremely slow growing, some much more rapid, depending on the type of corals that had made that section of sea their home. And the types of corals were amazingly varied: brain coral, elkhorn, staghorn, pillar. She fancied that the hard corals were the stonemasons of the reef, creating light and airy castles or massive round fortresses according to their whims.

At seventy feet, she could see the bottom. On an expanse of white sand were strewn a profusion of purple sea fans and whiplike red gorgonians — examples of soft coral. They sought the lower depths where they were safe from the wind and wave action that often whipped the sea's surface into a frenzy. At this depth they could slowly undulate and sway in the current, their delicate whips and fans bending this way and that as they sifted the water for food.

Yet for all the beauty of this world, she was fully aware of its dangers. The cuts from brushing against the coral two days earlier still stung. Coral cuts were generally slow to heal — little wonder, as they contained hundreds of little coral polyps, all angry at their displacement, all exuding their stinging toxins. The worst

— fire coral — was an innocuous looking clump of greenish gold about the size of a basketball, with separate leaves that looked very much like crumpled cabbage. One encounter with fire coral was enough to impress the animal's appearance upon a diver's brain forever.

She settled on the bottom and looked around. A four foot lemon shark flashed by like a silver bullet, its predator's mouth slightly agape, and she looked cautiously in the direction from which it had come. Nothing to worry about. If only her regulator would stop sticking. This was the third time it had given her trouble. Damn, Russ had said he would check it out. Hadn't he found time to look at it? She breathed shallowly, waiting for it to open up and deliver air without her having to make such an effort. Suddenly it was much easier to breathe. Gail sighed with relief. Maybe it would be all right now. She cleared some water out of her mask, wiggled her jaws a little, trying to find a less tiring position for the regulator between her teeth, and began to swim toward Battleship Reef.

The boys were hard at work when she arrived. Russ and Toshio had just finished fitting the yellow rope grid over the face of the reef and were flagging the sections to be probed. Brian and Grant were on their knees in the sand adjusting the air hammer, two streams of bubbles rising from their regulators. Russ and Toshio completed their job and backed off to kneel in the sand beside Brian and Grant. After a brief sign language discussion that Gail couldn't quite see, Brian and his buddy carried the air hammer to section nine. Grant held the heavy machine — a cross between a nail gun and a jackhammer — and Gail saw him nod. Brian pulled the trigger. She simultaneously heard and felt a low *poom*. A small cloud of debris rose from the hole the hammer had made in the reef, and Brian and Grant swam out of it, joining Russ and Toshio where they waited on the sand. She swam up to them, gave them the diver's okay sign — thumb and forefinger joined in a circle — and they all responded in kind. Maybe this operation would go smoothly after all.

She swam over to the reef, took the long metal probe out of its holder on her calf, a mountaineer's hammer from a pocket in her vest, and began to probe the reef. Her part of the operation was really very simple — if the air hammer had opened up a hole in the cavity, the probe would go in easily. If, however, no cavity existed, the probe would meet with immediate resistance. The tricky part, she had learned, was to be patient. Sometimes the small explosion made by the air hammer only loosened the material on top of the cavity. In those cases, some delicate probing and hammering was necessary to locate the cavity. But there was never any guarantee that her efforts would be successful. More often than not, all her patient work was met with failure — the risk taken by every scientist who ever lived. Would this be any different? Maybe. Presumably the computer knew *something*.

After fifteen minutes of careful probing and hammering, she admitted defeat. If there was a cavity in section nine, she couldn't find it. She checked her pressure gauge and frowned — almost a third of her air was gone already. She would have to work faster. Motioning for Brian and Grant to bring the air hammer, she swam over to where Russ and Toshio waited in the sand.

Toshio waved her down and she settled on the bottom beside him. Behind the plexiglass of his face mask, his brown eyes were worried. Pointing to Russ, he made the universal sign for diver in trouble — a throat slitting motion which meant he was having difficulty breathing.

Alarmed, Gail swam over to Russ. She made the okay sign, and he shrugged and returned it. She took her waterproof slate and grease pencil out of a pocket of her buoyancy compensator vest. "What's wrong?" she wrote.

He took the pencil and scribbled: "Sticky regulator valve. Intermittent trouble."

She looked at him, alarmed. The same trouble she had been having.

Russ took the slate again. "Toshio, too," he wrote.

That settled it. They were going up. Now.

Brian and Grant had just swum over to join them. Gail motioned with a thumb toward the surface. They looked at her in disbelief. Brian shook his head vehemently no, and Grant grabbed him and held him, nodding his head yes and pointing up. Finally Brian gave in, throwing down the air hammer in a fit of temper. In a swirl of sand and bubbles, he headed for the surface. Gail was dumbfounded. "Stop!" she shouted into her regulator. She needed Brian and Grant to buddy Russ and Toshio on the way up. It was absolutely necessary that one member of every team had a functioning regulator. But Brian had given her no choice. She motioned to Grant and sent him up after Brian. He nodded, picked up the air hammer, and began to ascend. She bit down on her regulator in frustration, vowing that when they reached the surface she would have some choice words for Brian. No one ever questioned a divemaster's judgment underwater.

She turned back to Russ and Toshio. Russ was already buddy breathing with Toshio. She felt a pang of alarm. What if Toshio's regulator, too, stuck shut? She reached behind her back, and released the second regulator of her octopus rig. Removing her own from her mouth, she clamped her teeth on the new one, cleared the water, and took a breath. Or tried to. To her horror, nothing

98

happened. The octopus rig was dead. It was clear to her now that the malfunctioning regulators were no accident. Someone had sabotaged them. But who? And why? Grimly, she vowed to find out. But first, she had to get Russ, Toshio, and herself safely to the surface.

She spat out the octopus regulator, replaced it with her own, cleared it, and gingerly took a breath. She was truly terrified that it might not work. But it did. Air flooded into her mouth, and it was only a great effort of will that prevented her from gulping mouthfuls of it.

She swam over to Toshio and Russ, noting what a contrast to Brian and Grant they made. In trouble, and no doubt anxious and apprehensive, still they had waited for the divemaster to give them permission to ascend. She felt fury in her heart at the mysterious saboteur. Did he know that he had placed their lives in danger? This wasn't just a little joke on Jinx Team — this was attempted murder.

She motioned Russ and Toshio to her. "Trouble," she wrote on the slate. "We may all end up breathing off one regulator. So we need to go up together. Okay?"

They nodded, eyes frightened. Her heart went out to them. They were just kids. They made a circle, facing in, arms linked, and began to ascend. Gail looked up at the surface. A little over sixty feet, she judged. Two pressure changes. They'd have to go slowly if they didn't want to risk the bends or an air embolism. "Okay?" she asked them, thumb and forefinger joined.

"Okay," they responded, Toshio waiting patiently for Russ to return his regulator, Russ taking the regulation two breaths that buddy breathing allowed.

At forty feet, the water became noticeably warmer. Gail's regulator stopped working. Perhaps it was the temperature difference. She cursed and tapped Toshio's arm. He hesitated only a moment, nodded, took two deep breaths, and handed over the regulator. She looked straight into Russ' eyes, and he bravely made the okay sign at her as he waited for air. She took her two breaths, handed the regulator to Russ, and looked over at Toshio. He seemed the same as always — calm, implacable. She said a prayer of thanks for his unruffled, dependable nature. Three on a regulator would never work with someone like Brian. In SCUBA classes she had taught, for a graduation exercise she had shared one regulator with six or seven students. But that had been in a shallow swimming pool, under supervised conditions. This was life or death.

At thirty feet the water was warmer still, and much brighter. She looked at her watch. As long as they exhaled on the way up, they could swim up from here. The danger of the bends had passed. She tapped Toshio and Russ to let her out of the circle, and began a free ascent, leaving them with the regulator. As she kicked past them, she noted that they were continuing their slow, steady ascent. Toshio was even looking at his watch. Good for him. If their air lasted, she was willing to bet he'd keep them at ten feet for ten minutes — the classic safety margin.

She exhaled slowly, following her bubbles to the surface, and when her head broke the water, she began to inflate her vest. A quick check of the horizon showed her that they would have quite a swim to the boat — almost a quarter of a mile. Her heart sank. What were Grant and Brian doing, anyhow? Why hadn't they spotted her? A terrible thought occurred to her: what if something had happened to them?

"Hey!" she yelled in the direction of the boat. She waved her arms over her head and yelled again. Finally, miraculously, someone answered. A faint shout came from the boat, and she could see the white blur of a T-shirt being waved back and forth.

Russ and Toshio surfaced beside her, Russ gasping and choking. Toshio held Russ' head out of the water and inflated his vest while Russ got his breathing under control.

"Brother!" he exclaimed when he was able to stop coughing. "I thought we were goners there for a few minutes."

"We might well have been," Gail said. "I think we have Toshio to thank."

Toshio rinsed his mask and looked embarrassed. "I suggest we proceed to the boat," he said. "I, for one, have had quite enough swimming for one day. I would appreciate putting something solid and dry under my feet. Dr. Murray, shall I lead or follow?"

* * * * *

"I don't get it." Russ slumped on his bed and tossed a crumpled beer can in the direction of the waste basket. "I checked those regulators myself."

"I looked at them, too," Toshio said mournfully. "Once before, one of the other divemasters played a little joke on us. As I recall, he made a slight adjustment to the O-rings in our regulators." He shrugged philosophically. "Of course, the joke was discovered almost at once, as the regulators leaked streams of air. So no harm was done."

"This was a little different," Gail said grimly. "A lot of harm might have been done. If it was another joke, someone has a pretty warped sense of humor. And if it wasn't a joke . . ." She was reluctant to state the obvious.

Toshio sighed. "It's the bonus," he said. "Sloat has planted the seeds of avarice in everyone's mind."

"Not everyone's," Russ objected. "The bonus hasn't made *us* crazy."

"Well, perhaps not totally," Toshio agreed wryly.

"Toshio," she said, "did you just say a *divemaster* tampered with your O-rings last time?"

Toshio nodded. "It was common knowledge at the time, but of course there was no way to prove it."

"Who?" she demanded.

Toshio and Russ looked at each other.

"Don't give me that macho male code of silence. You know how serious this is."

Toshio sighed. "Alec Evans. Sloat's favorite student."

She should have guessed. Alec Evans was the divemaster who had been so rude to her this morning in Miss Liszt's office. Well, Sloat was going to get an earful about the fun-loving Mr. Evans.

"Can I take it that we're not diving tomorrow?" Russ asked. "I think I'd like to get drunk. Sort of a celebration of still being alive. And then I think I'd like to sleep the clock around."

Gail laughed a little bitterly. "No, we're not diving tomorrow, so you can get as drunk as you want. In fact, we're not diving again at all until I get a few things straight."

"That suits me," Russ said. "Things do seem to be getting a little out of hand."

"I'll see you two later," she said, standing. "I'm going to see Sloat. Or try to see him. And then I think I might go into town and get drunk myself. Any suggestions?"

Russ said, "You might try the Club Caribe. It's on that street just south of the main drag, by the water. It has a nice patio overlooking the ocean. And there's always a loud band playing. So you can brood outdoors in the dark or dance the night away to the strains of wild reggae."

In spite of her anger and depression, she smiled. "The Club Caribe will suit me just fine."

"Ah, but *which* you?" Toshio asked.

"The brooding me," she told him. "I have a lot of brooding to do."

"Sloat?" Toshio guessed.

"Among other things, Sloat," she said.

Chapter 8

She found a table on the outdoor patio, ordered an Amstel beer, and gazed morosely out at the quickly darkening ocean. Had there been a green flash tonight when the sun went down? She smiled ruefully. If there had been, she was glad she had missed it. It would only have reminded her of Marike.

Late this afternoon, after unsuccessful attempts to locate Sloat, Alec Evans, or Brian and Grant, she had given up. Returning to her room, she had sat on her bed in the growing gloom, trying her best not to let depression overtake her, and trying hard not to think of Marike.

Everything was going wrong. Then, with a stab of guilt, she remembered she hadn't gotten back to the computer room to call up her program and have a look at it. If Charlie Henderson had gotten into her files, she needed to know what had happened. If he had run the program, it would now be gibberish. Well, checking it out would have to wait for another day. She was too tired, too anxious, too depressed, and too angry to give the task the concentration it deserved. Maybe Russ had had the best idea after all — get drunk and go to bed. She had decided to follow his example.

She took another swallow of her beer and tried to empty her mind. Inside the club, the enthusiastic reggae band finished a set. Here on the patio in the darkness, things were relatively quiet. Most of the patrons seemed to prefer being inside, dancing and drinking. Candles in amber glass holders on the tables provided the only light, and she felt hidden, safe, and anonymous. She closed her eyes and leaned back in her chair, willing herself to relax. A breeze had sprung up, and its gentle fingers rustled the fronds of the palm trees lining the patio, lifting her hair and making the candle gutter. Only three other tables were occupied. From one of them came a woman's throaty, intimate laughter — a dusky, velvet sound that filled Gail with sudden longing. Closing her eyes, she realized how intensely she longed for someone to sit beside her in the summer darkness, someone to whisper to, someone to laugh with. The emotion was so powerful that she wondered how she could bear it. But it passed, and in its wake she felt drained, hopeless, and afraid.

Panic gripped her then, and she felt the urge to flee, to run away. But she had nothing and no one to run to. There was no one waiting for her anywhere. No one thought of her with love, or longing, or regret. No one counted the days until her return. I exist nowhere but here in this place, now, in this moment, she told herself, and the thought terrified her. How did I get to be so alone, she wondered. How do these things happen?

"Hello, Gail," a quiet voice said. "May I join you for a moment?"

She turned. The light from the club's open doorway made a bright halo of Marike's hair. She wore white slacks and a white shirt with a pleated front, open to the third button, the sleeves rolled casually above her elbows, exposing her tanned arms. The effect was stunning. In the dim light she seemed to glow from within: golden skin, emerald eyes, silver hair, all radiating light. "Sit down," Gail said, her throat tight.

Marike sat, hands clasped in front of her, staring at the candle. Gail saw that she was in distress, but the memory of their last conversation kept her from speaking.

"I'm being sued by those jackasses we pulled out of the Atlantic the other day," Marike said.

"But I thought . . ." Gail said, then stopped. To say more would reveal she had eavesdropped on Marike and Rolf.

Marike was too angry to notice. "That's typical male appreciation for you! We save their lives and they take me to court. Negligence, they claim."

"That's ridiculous," Gail said heatedly. "No one held a gun to their heads to make them go diving. And I heard the radio conversation you had with Peter — it's obvious they meant to go off by themselves. I don't see how they could ever hope to win a lawsuit against you."

"Well, I'm sure they don't want to go to court any more than I do," Marike said. "They're trying to intimidate me into a quick out-of-court settlement." She shrugged. "We're playing chicken."

"How much do they want?" Gail asked.

Marike waved a hand impatiently. "Too much. Ten, twelve thousand dollars. Something like that." She ran a hand through her hair and exhaled audibly. "Listen," she said, "I have no right to ask this of you after my self-righteous little speech, but if you would do something for me, it would be a big help." She looked directly at Gail, and in that instant Gail knew she would do whatever was asked of her. What a fool she'd been, she chided herself.

"What do you want me to do?" Did her voice sound unsteady?

"Go to see Rolf Klee. Give him a statement. Tell him what you overheard, then what happened during the dive. That jerk tried to kill you, you know. Make sure Rolf knows that." She smiled a little crookedly. "I need all the help I can get on this. If word gets around that Osten's Bay isn't a safe SCUBA lodge, my business will be finished. Osten's Bay is as much my dream as it was my father's, Gail. And I won't go down without a fight."

"I'll do whatever I can," she said. "I'd like to help."

Marike heaved a sigh. "Thank you," she said quietly. Then after a moment, she raised her eyes to Gail's. "Listen, I was completely out of line the other morning. What I said was, well, perfectly rotten. I guess I overreact whenever the subject of the Institute comes up." In the dim light, her eyes smoldered. "I accused you before I had any right. Maybe you're not one of them. Maybe you're different. Maybe you're not in league with Sloat." She put a hand on the table, and Gail had to restrain herself from reaching over to take it.

"I'm certainly not in league with Sloat," Gail told her. "And judging from my popularity around the Institute, nobody thinks I'm one of them."

A burst of raucous laughter came from inside the club, followed by the squawk of electric guitars being tuned. "Is there someplace else we can talk?" Gail asked. "There are things going on at the Institute that don't seem right." She laughed a little ruefully. "I really would appreciate being able to talk to someone."

Marike looked around. "Well, there's little point in moving down the terrace. This reggae stuff really carries." She thought for a moment. "Why don't we pick up some beer, take my jeep, and drive down the coast to Karpata? You may have missed the green flash, but with any luck you'll get to see the moon come up."

"All right," Gail said, amazing herself by the coolness of her tone. "I'd like that. Why don't I pick up the beer at the bar and meet you in the parking lot?"

* * * * *

"It's beautiful," Gail exclaimed. The moon had edged into view over the rim of the ocean, making a rippled ribbon of silver from the horizon to their feet. She waded a little farther into the water, bending to catch a handful of light. "I'm a little drunk," she told Marike, "so pardon me if I'm silly."

"Be as silly as you want," Marike told her. "You have good cause."

Gail had spent the last hour talking about the "accident" with the regulators, the mysterious assignment as divemaster, ISAUR's sudden possession of a cavity location program, and Benjamin Sloat's eccentric behavior. Marike had listened gravely to it all, agreeing there were odd things happening at ISAUR but unable, as Gail had been, to offer any suggestion that might tie them all together. And now Gail found she was incredibly tired of thinking about the Institute, Benjamin Sloat, diving — all of it. Her brain was buzzing, and she wanted to empty it of all thoughts of ISAUR. This beautiful night was inexorably passing, and she didn't want to spend it talking, or even thinking, about the Institute.

"Thank you for listening to me blather on about ISAUR," she said, "but I'd rather enjoy the night and the sea. Tonight is too beautiful to squander."

She felt rather than heard Marike come up behind her. "All right," Marike said softly. "Whatever you like." Marike put a hand on her shoulder and Gail stood perfectly still. "You know," Marike said, "I had another reason for suggesting we leave the club and come here to talk."

"Oh?" Gail said, her voice unsteady. She turned slowly to Marike.

"Yes," Marike said quietly. "I gave a lot of thought to what we should have said to each other the morning you left." She laughed a little bitterly. "The morning I drove you away is more like it. And I've also been thinking about what you said the night before. You evidently wanted more time." She took her hand from Gail's shoulder. "I rushed you, and I'm sorry. It's my nature — I'm impatient." She swallowed audibly, and Gail suddenly realized Marike was as nervous as she was. "I acted very badly," Marike said. "Not listening to what you were trying to tell me that night and jumping to conclusions about the Institute the next morning. I'm sorry, Gail. Very sorry. Will you forgive me?"

Gail closed her eyes. Was this really happening? She had all but given up trying to imagine a reconciliation.

Yet here it was. She drew a deep breath. "Yes," she said, her voice quavering a little. "But only if you'll let me say something first. Something I need to say."

"Of course," Marike said. "What is it?"

"I'm a coward," Gail said simply. "And it's not something I'm proud of."

Marike raised her eyebrows. "A coward? You? It's not possible."

"Yes it is," Gail said. "I've been a coward all my life. I'm afraid of everything. Of not succeeding. Of succeeding. Of other people. Of what those other people might think of me. But most of all, I'm afraid of myself. Of my feelings. Of what might happen to me if I ever acknowledged I have feelings and that I can trust them." She raised a hand to caress Marike's cheek. "In the past day or two I've been thinking about that. What's the worst that could happen, I asked myself. Well, I suppose I might get hurt." She shrugged. "It's not a happy thought. A bruised heart mends a whole lot more slowly than a coral cut. And I've protected my heart pretty well in the last few years. Maybe too well," she said quietly. "All it's gotten me is alone. Maybe it's time to start taking some chances."

"I won't hurt you," Marike said, putting her hands on Gail's hips. "At least not intentionally. Take all the time you need. Please believe me — I'm not toying with you. I'm serious. I don't do things like this lightly. And I don't think you're a coward at all. I think you're very honest." She bent to kiss Gail's cheek. "Take all the time you need to be comfortable with me. I can wait." She held out her hand. Smiling, Gail took it. "Let's walk to the next cove," Marike said. "We might have to wade through some deep water, but the bottom's sandy. Come on."

Arms around each other's waists, they walked along the beach, over the cool, wet, hard-packed sand, then down toward the water. "Here," Marike said, pointing to a large clump of boulders that had long ago fallen from the cliff behind them and now blocked their way. "We have to wade out into the water to get around these. I think if we roll our pants up above our knees we won't get wet. And we're between tides, so we don't need to worry about the current."

Hand in hand they entered the water. As it rose above her ankles, then over her calves, Gail marveled again at how exciting the sea was at night. It was as warm as blood. Suddenly she understood why she had always been drawn to the ocean. In its contrasts — creator and destroyer, nurturer and killer — it was essentially female. It was Kali, the Hindu goddess of creation and destruction. And she understood, too, why men feared the sea. It was a mystery akin to the mystery of woman. Was this why the sea had never frightened her — because they were part of each other?

She rounded the half-submerged clump of boulders and waded out of the water, up the beach, and onto the dry sand of the little cove. Turning to look out at the dark sky sprinkled with stars, the rippled black water, the silver trail of moonlight, she was intoxicated. But certainly not from the alcohol. No, she was drunk on the beauty of the night. On sea and moonlight. And on Marike.

Marike sat on the beach, arms clasped around her knees, looking out at the dark, moonlit water. Gail stood on the sand, silent, perfectly happy. The Institute and its problems seemed a thousand miles away. Here in this little cove there was only the sea, the moon, and the two of them. She looked over at Marike, a dark silhouette against the moon, and a feeling of déjà vu came over her. Have I been here before, she asked herself. But it wasn't the place that teased her memory. It was the person. Marike. She blinked, uncertain, and suddenly an image came into focus, an image only reluctantly surrendered by memory, an image of a woman kneeling in the moonlight, raising her arms to the moon. Gail froze, transfixed.

"Gail," Marike said, and raised her arms, reaching for her.

Beginning to shiver, Gail closed her eyes. The dream, she told herself, this is a scene from my dream. Exactly as I dreamed it. And the woman in my dream, the woman who led me down to the sea, who knelt in the moonlight and reached for me — that woman is right there in front of me. Opening her eyes, she knelt unsteadily and took Marike's hands in hers.

"What is it?" Marike asked. "You look frightened."

Gail shook her head. "Not frightened exactly. Awed, maybe." She squeezed Marike's hands a little. "Do you know what I'd like?"

"What?"

"I'd like you to hold me."

Marike encircled her with her arms. "Tell me what's wrong. Please?"

"There's nothing wrong," Gail whispered, her lips against Marike's face. "Just talk to me. Convince me you're real and not a dream, someone I imagined."

Marike laughed. "You're not dreaming. I'm no figment of your imagination." She held Gail close. "I'll tell you the story of my life. Maybe that will convince you I'm flesh and blood. No dream lover could have a life half as ordinary as mine." She stretched her long legs out in front of her and lay down with a sigh. "Come here," she said. "Let's lie together and look at the stars. Now, where shall I start?"

But even with Marike's soft voice in her ears, the wonder of suddenly finding herself in the midst of a scene from her dreams would not leave Gail. Who are you, Marike Osten, she asked silently. And who put you into my dreams? Was all this presdestined? Are we just acting out parts in a play written by someone else? By some higher power? She shook her head. No, she wasn't a fatalist. But what then did the dream mean? She turned toward Marike and propped her head on one hand. Yes, that face, that beautiful, sensitive face, was the face of the woman in her dreams. No doubt about it. She raised a tentative hand and traced Marike's eyebrows.

Marike stopped talking and closed her eyes, sighing. "Are you convinced I'm real?" she asked softly.

"Yes," Gail said. "I think I am. But perhaps it doesn't matter. If this is a dream, we're both in it." She smiled, tracing the outline of Marike's lips. "But I have to admit you feel real to me."

Marike kissed Gail's fingertips and rolled on her side to face her. She raised a hand to stroke Gail's hair, then put her hand against Gail's cheek. Gail closed her eyes. It all seemed so *right*. And suddenly she knew what she wanted.

"Make love to me, Marike," she whispered.

"Are you sure?"

"I'm sure." And she was. Absolutely. She took Marike's hand from her cheek, turned it over, and kissed the palm. Marike murmured and, emboldened, Gail leaned over and pressed her mouth to Marike's. It felt strange to take the lead, but exciting, too. "I'm sure," she repeated. Sensing the other woman's hesitance, she brushed her lips across Marike's again, feeling the gentle pressure as Marike responded.

Then Marike seemed to understand that she truly had been given permission to proceed, and she put her arms around Gail, burying her face in Gail's hair, holding her tightly.

"But I don't want to rush," Gail told her, a little embarrassed. "This is very special to me. Do you understand?"

Marike nodded. "I do. I want to please you, so stop me if I'm not doing things right. Promise?"

"I promise," Gail said shakily. "But you do please me, Marike. I'm sorry if I seem eccentric."

"You're not eccentric. Isn't there some proverb about pleasure prolonged being sweeter?"

Gail laughed a little. "If there isn't, there should be."

"All right, then," Marike said, her hands brushing Gail's hair off her face. She drew Gail's face down to hers and kissed her, her lips at first soft as moths' wings. Then Marike parted Gail's lips with her own, her tongue gently probing, questing, and Gail felt again the sweet stab of pleasure she had felt when Marike had kissed her that night at Osten's Bay. But then it had been wrong. Opportunistic. Tonight was different. Tonight was right.

Marike's lips trailed softly down Gail's cheek to her chin, and then she was kissing her ear, creating a delicious hot, deep agony. Gasping, Gail moved her head and met Marike's mouth with her own. And this time it was her tongue that sought Marike's, her arms that tightened around the other woman.

Marike moved in Gail's arms and drew her up to lie on top of her, her legs between Gail's. Gail moaned a little as Marike slid her warm hand up under her shirt, caressing the planes of her back. Marike kissed Gail's cheek and throat, and Gail murmured in pleasure.

"Sit up," Marike said. When Gail sat up with her legs straddling Marike's, Marike lifted Gail's shirt over her head, dropping it beside them on the sand. With a few quick movements she unbuttoned her own and tossed it aside. Marike raised her arms to Gail, her fingers trailing lightly over Gail's arms and shoulders, making her shiver. Her fingers rested for a moment on Gail's bare throat. Then, very slowly, Marike brushed the backs of her hands over Gail's breasts. Gail gasped as Marike cupped each breast in a warm palm. "So beautiful," she breathed. She brought her mouth to Gail's breasts, tasting each nipple delicately with her tongue, then taking each gently in her teeth. Gail thought she would faint from pleasure. "I want to feel you against me," Marike said. "All of you." Her hands brushed Gail's stomach. "Let's take the rest of these clothes off."

A moment later Gail lay naked in Marike's arms, the whole warm length of Marike's body pressed to hers.

"Oh, Gail," Marike said into Gail's hair. "I want you so much." She kissed Gail's forehead and laid her gently on the sand, then propped herself on one arm, looking down at her. Bending to kiss Gail's breasts, she brushed her other hand over her stomach and thighs and Gail began to tremble. Desire ignited in her like a flame, and she raised her hips to Marike's hand. "Lovely," Marike murmured, her lips on Gail's nipples.

Gail moaned as Marike's hand glided over her body, finally coming to rest between her legs. Involuntarily, she moved a little, and Marike's hand began to stroke the soft inner skin of her thighs. Gail trembled and moved a little more as Marike's hand continued its seeking, finally coming to rest in a place that made Gail's breath catch in her throat. Then Gail felt Marike hesitate, and suddenly delay was unbearable. Taking Marike's hand, she guided it to where she wanted it, where she had longed to have it that night at Osten's Bay. Marike moaned, and Gail felt her questing fingers glide inside her. Pleasure pierced her — a pleasure almost beyond enduring — and she closed her thighs, holding Marike's hand still.

"Wait, Marike," she whispered shakily. "Please."

"It's all right," Marike murmured, kissing Gail's closed eyelids. "It's all right. Just tell me when."

Gail gasped, struggling to breathe, feeling Marike inside her. At any moment she might faint from the intensity of her sensations — a slow, molten rippling of pleasure. But though she waited, the intensity did not diminish. Instead, it grew. The red molten rippling became a white hot, urgent ache, a heat that ran along her veins, an ache whose center was Marike's hand. It was the most agonizing sweetness she had ever felt. "Marike," she gasped, her arms gripping Marike's shoulders.

Marike understood. She began to stroke, to move her fingers, and all at once, against her closed eyelids, Gail saw starbursts of bright light as the surge of pleasure rapidly crested, becoming an incandescent tidal wave of ecstasy. She cried out, feeling herself tighten helplessly around Marike's fingers in shudders as rhythmic and powerful as waves breaking on the seashore. She clung to Marike as the waves ebbed, her body shaken every now and then by a retreating tide that finally left her spent and trembling in Marike's arms.

"Gail," Marike said softly, kissing her cheek. "Gail."

Gail sighed in answer, kissing Marike softly, but it was a long time before she opened her eyes.

Marike smiled. "Hello."

Gail sighed again and put a hand on Marike's cheek. "Hello yourself." Marike kissed her palm, and Gail took a deep breath. "You know," she told Marike hesitantly, shyly, "you may have to tell me what you like. I'm not very practiced at this sort of thing."

Marike laughed. "I don't know — you may surprise yourself. This sort of thing comes rather naturally, don't you think? I'm not very practiced either. But if I have to tell you what to do, I will." She kissed Gail's nose. "When the time comes, that is. Right now, however, we have a little problem. Look."

Gail looked at the sea in alarm. While they had made love, the tide had come in. The sea hissed into foam on the beach. They would soon have to wade back to the cove where they had started, or be cut off. "I see," she said, sitting up. "We'll have to swim if we wait any longer."

Marike helped her to her feet. "You're right." Scooping up Gail's clothes, she handed them over. "I wish this evening could have a more romantic conclusion, but we'll have to dress and run."

Gail pulled on her clothes, one eye on the incoming tide.

"Come on," Marike said, holding out a hand. Smiling, Gail took it. Marike kissed her fingers, once, quickly.

"It was wonderful," Gail said.

Marike squeezed her fingers. "I hope you know now that I'm serious."

Gail nodded. "Yes, I know that now." She took a deep breath. "How about tomorrow night? Or rather, tonight?"

Marike kissed Gail's hand again. "I was hoping you'd suggest something like that. Only let's meet in someplace a little warmer and more comfortable. How does Osten's Bay sound?"

"Fine." Gail smiled. "It sounds fine."

"Could you drive up after work?"

"I could. And I'd like to very much."

"All right," Marike said. "Let's get out of here."

Gail took a look at the black, foaming water. "All right, I'm ready. Let's go."

Chapter 9

Gail reached the Institute as the sun was rising. She looked at her watch. Almost six a.m. The diving teams would have left by now. That meant Sloat should be in his office, ready to begin another day. She set her lips in a grim line, thinking of the confrontation. As she wheeled the jeep into the parking lot, she took a quick look at the Institute's dock and noted with some surprise that none of the dive boats had left. Odd, she thought. What could have delayed the dive teams? Slamming the jeep's door, she hurried across the parking lot and down the path to Sloat's office.

"Dr. Murray!" an urgent voice called.

She turned to see Russ loping along the path behind her. "What's going on?" she asked him.

Russ shook his head. "No one's diving today. Sloat called everything off this morning. Most of the divers went back to bed, but Toshio and I have been nosing around and have managed to find out a few things."

"Like what?" Gail asked, torn between wanting to know what was going on and wanting to corner Benjamin Sloat before he slithered away again.

"Marvin — the little nerd who mother hens the electronic gear — Sloat, and a so-called computer genius from DARDCO, were up all night in the communications dome, working with the computer." He snorted. "Must have been something pretty important to make Sloat miss his sleep."

Gail's stomach clenched. "Do you know what they were up to?"

Russ shook his head. "Not exactly. But Toshio heard they were working on the cavity location program. Apparently they've just now gotten the bugs worked out of it. Seems as though they made some kind of breakthrough last night. Oh, and by the way, just before they started all this heavy computing, Sloat was asking for you. He was pretty upset."

A seed of suspicion sprouted in Gail's mind. "He was? Why?"

Russ frowned. "He was all bent out of shape because you hadn't downloaded some data, or at least left your passwords with someone."

"Oh," Gail said, only half listening. So Sloat had wanted her passwords, had he? "Listen, Russ, I want to catch Sloat before he runs off somewhere," she said. "He and I have to discuss some things. I'll talk to you later."

She hurried along the path, conscious that she was dressed in the same clothes she had worn the night before, except this morning they were sandy and watermarked. Well, it couldn't be helped. Her appearance wouldn't make a bit of difference this morning. She made a bet with herself that Sloat wouldn't even notice. So Sloat had wanted her passwords. To do what? Simply to take a look at her data files in her absence? After all, he had asked her to be sure to download them. Or was he up to something less innocent? Was it conceivable that Sloat, and not Charlie Henderson, had burgled her files and helped himself to a look at her cavity location program? He could have — she had given Miss Liszt Erindale's computer codes months ago.

She tried to control her fury. Was Sloat's sudden lack of interest in the contribution she might make to ISAUR's fledgling cavity location research due to her sudden redundancy? After all, if he already had her program, why did he need her?

A horrifying thought occurred to her, and she stopped dead in her tracks. No. It just wasn't possible. She swallowed, looking apprehensively at the path to Sloat's office. Had he assigned her the job of divemaster precisely because it *was* high risk? And the accident with the regulators — was it possible they had been ordered by Sloat, and not engineered by some avaricious divemaster?

She clenched her fists. It all fit. But if her theory was correct, then she had best proceed very cautiously with Benjamin Sloat. She took a deep breath and continued walking.

As soon as she rounded the corner by the clump of palm trees and approached the dome where Sloat's office was located, she knew something was wrong. The door to the outer office stood half open — something Miss Liszt would never allow. Frowning, she pushed the door fully open and stepped inside. Miss Liszt was nowhere to be seen. And from inside Sloat's office came a masculine buzz of voices — perhaps two other people besides Sloat. They seemed excited and pleased, and one of them broke into laughter at a comment Sloat made. What was going on?

A familiar form edged backwards out of Sloat's office, called a hesitant goodbye, turned, and hurried toward her, head down. It was Marvin, the communications technician. She moved to intercept him.

"Marvin," she said, "I hear congratulations are in order."

Marvin stopped and raised his head, adjusting his glasses and peering at her myopically. "Well, yes," he admitted. Evidently it didn't occur to him to wonder how she knew about his accomplishment.

"No need to be modest," Gail told him. "After all, the man who worked the bugs out of ISAUR's cavity location program is deserving of a little respect. Right?"

"Right, right," Marvin agreed hastily. "Except for one thing." He looked down at his shoes. "I'm, well, that is, you're congratulating the wrong person."

"The wrong person?" Gail exclaimed. "But who else has the expertise to accomplish such a thing?"

Marvin cleared his throat. "No one," he told her, looking ashamed. "Not the computer expertise. Although Williams did help a little. And Dr. Sloat." Hearing a laugh from Sloat's office, he looked furtively over his shoulder.

She saw anxiety in his eyes. This was a frightened little man.

"In fact, they did it all," Marvin continued. "The whole thing. I mean Williams did it. I hardly helped at all." His bloodshot blue eyes looked bitterly at Gail. "Williams. DARDCO's computer genius. He doesn't know

RAM from ROM." Suddenly seeming to remember his lines, he shifted gears again. "Good old Williams. He did it." He blinked, trying to communicate to Gail something beyond words. "I'm sorry. Really sorry. But I have to go now."

"Wait, Marvin," she called after him. But it was too late.

Sloat emerged from his office, trailed by a younger, sandy-haired man in khaki pants and an orange polo shirt with a DARDCO logo on one breast. When Sloat saw her he looked as guilty as a kid caught with his hand in the cookie jar.

Later, she realized that was the moment when she knew, intuitively, what was going on. How all the pieces fit together. Who were the bad guys and who the good. But her scientific, rational mind resisted such knowledge. The truth was too enormous and too terrible. Her rational mind balked, refusing to credit the truth glimpsed by her unconscious. It demanded proof. It resisted condemning without more evidence; therefore, it continued to accumulate facts, to attempt to sift the essential from the unimportant. And so the moment passed. Later, she would look back in regret. Had she paid attention to her unconscious, she would have turned and run. Instead, she forged ahead, ignoring the alarms going off in her mind.

"Ah, Gail," Sloat said, as if she were the very person he had been wanting to see. "You know, I was just talking about you to Williams here." He slapped the other man on the back, and Williams gave her a dutiful smile.

"Mr. Williams," Gail said carefully, not quite sure how to play this role. "I'm Dr. Murray. I was hired to perfect the Institute's cavity locating program, but I see you've beaten us to it. Dr. Sloat told me that you — pardon me, someone — had developed a cavity location

123

program, but that it had a few glitches in it still. He mentioned that you might need me to help render it fully operational. But I see that you've managed to work out the problems." She could hardly keep the bitterness out of her voice. "Congratulations."

Williams looked sidelong at Sloat, evidently wondering exactly what to say. When Sloat offered no assistance, he grinned and responded. "Well, thank you," he told her. Then, as if in afterthought, he added: "No hard feelings, I hope?"

Gail forced herself to laugh. "Well, maybe a few. Being upstaged is never pleasant, but I suppose I can live with it." She looked pointedly at Sloat. "I gather that you won't be needing me to download my program now."

Sloat raised his eyebrows, groomed his beard furiously, and pretended to give the question some thought. "Well, it does seem a little superfluous, doesn't it? I don't know — what do you think, Williams?"

Williams shrugged. "I think we'd just be wasting Dr. Murray's valuable time. After all, we've got the answer, so we really don't need to reinvent the wheel, now do we?"

"Whatever you like," Gail said. "I suppose I'll have other duties now that you don't need me to work on the cavity program. We should have a talk about the dive teams, don't you think, Dr. Sloat?"

Sloat blinked rapidly. "The dive teams?" He sounded as though he had never heard of them.

"Yes," Gail said. "The dive teams. Presumably we'll continue to test your cavity program. I know I collected data for years when I was trying to perfect mine. But we can talk about that when you're finished with Mr. Williams." She was consumed with curiosity. Just how far did Sloat intend to take this charade?

"Oh, we're finished now," Williams said, trying a charming smile. Gail looked at him expressionlessly, and his smile faded. "See you tonight, then Benjamin," he said, heading for the door.

"Oh, right," Sloat replied distractedly. "And be sure to wear your tux. The press conference will be televised."

"You can count on me," Williams said, winking conspiratorially, closing the door to the outer office quietly behind him.

Press conference? Gail's heart sank.

Sloat turned to her, his expression one of avuncular concern. "My dear young woman," he said, shaking his head. Compassion fairly dripped from his voice. "This is such a happy day for us, but a day fraught with such disappointment for you." He shook his head. "Such disappointment. Please, my dear, do come and sit down."

"I'd rather not," Gail told him. "So Williams did it, did he? He must be the programmer you couldn't tell me about. I notice he works for DARDCO."

"Mmmm, yes," Sloat replied. "DARDCO will of course be sharing the program's application with us. I'll announce that tonight."

"Of course," Gail said, her composure slipping. "A perfect example of science and industry working together for the common good."

Sloat cocked his head. "I couldn't have said it better myself," he said.

"So there's to be a press conference? So soon?" she asked. "Are you absolutely sure the program works?" She shook her head in feigned thoughtfulness. "It might be a little premature."

Sloat's brown eyes stared back at her, opaque, expressionless. She ignored the chill feeling on the back of her neck and plunged on.

"I wouldn't have thought such an esoteric area of marine geology as cavity location would merit so much fanfare. It certainly didn't at Erindale," she remarked.

"Ah, well, DARDCO's R and D arm has always been interested in cavities," Sloat muttered. "Incidentally," he said, lowering his voice to an intimate level, "may I assume that you'll be coming to the press conference?"

"Why, thank you," she told him. "But I probably won't be there. I just haven't a thing to wear."

"Mmmm," he said thoughtfully, his eyes searching her face.

"We need to talk about the diving teams," she said, changing the subject.

"Ah yes," Sloat replied. "The diving teams." He held up a hand. "Before you start, let me just say that I heard about what happened yesterday, and I assure you that appropriate disciplinary measures have been taken."

"They have?" Gail asked.

Sloat nodded. "Another practical joke on Jinx Team, so I was told."

"Oh?" Gail remarked sarcastically. "That practical joke could have gotten one of us seriously injured. And I'm beginning to wonder how much of a joke it really was."

Sloat fixed her with a look of warning, and Gail's heart beat faster. He was certainly guilty — it showed all over his face. But guilty of what? "My dear, I know you're upset," Sloat said. "By what happened to your dive team as well as by what happened to your research project. It's been a difficult few days. But it's important to keep one's perspective. To look at the big picture. And we can't let ourselves be swept away by our emotions, now can we? After all, you're still a scientist and a fellow of this Institute. I expect you to behave like one and not let petty jealousy get the better of you. Bear up, Dr. Murray, bear up."

Sloat was attempting to shift the emphasis of events in order to make *her* feel guilty. The man was a master of manipulation. Be careful, Gail, she told herself. Be indignant, but not too indignant. "Oh, I'll bear up," she told him. "Petty jealousy is not one of the emotions likely to get the better of me. But I want you to know that if I ever get any proof that Alec Evans tampered with our regulators, I'll press charges against him. Criminal charges. Make no mistake about that. And you'll have to get another divemaster. I'm finished."

Sloat stared at her impassively. Then he shrugged, an elaborate, dramatic gesture. "If you insist, Dr. Murray," he said, shaking his head sadly. "If you insist."

"Oh, I do insist," she told him.

They looked at each other. There was nothing further to be gained by talking to him. She really did want to know what duties he planned to assign her in the future, but now was not the time to discuss them. There would be plenty of time for that later, once she had ascertained the truth.

"You know, I'd be very interested in taking a look at Williams' cavity location program. I'm assuming I'll be able to do that?"

Sloat spread his arms in an expansive gesture. "Yes, of course. In fact I want you to."

She fought to keep her composure. Was there no end to this man's duplicity?

Sloat shook his head in bemusement. "You're ISAUR's expert. Williams is DARDCO's. Even though ISAUR will be sharing the program, we want to make sure that it's as good as it can possibly be." He waved a hand. "Of course we know it works, but we want to make sure that it works efficiently. Every time. That's where I see your contribution being made."

"You do?" Gail asked, too amazed to do anything but stare.

"Definitely," Sloat said, looking at her solemnly. "And you know, Dr. Murray, I have to agree with you about the dive teams."

"You do?"

"Yes," he said, shaking his head sorrowfully. "You're much too valuable to risk to adolescent underwater pranks. If you hadn't communicated to me your reluctance to go on with the diving program, I'd have forbidden you to continue taking part."

Gail was incredulous. The man was unbelievable! Was she really expected to swallow this sudden concern for her welfare? She hardly knew how to respond. Just play the game, she told herself.

"I'm certainly glad you've come to see things my way," she said.

"Oh I have. Indeed I have," he said. "Now, if you don't mind, I have a lot of work to do to get ready for the press conference tonight." He smiled and turned back toward his office. "Oh, and please do try to be there. Despite what you said, I know you'll find something appropriate to wear. Women always do. Can I count on it?" He smiled charmingly at her, displaying white, even teeth.

"Yes, I think you can," she told him. She'd like to be on hand after all she decided. Perhaps at the press conference Sloat would explain why a second-tier oil company and a tiny research institute thought this new cavity location program such hot news. In fact, she couldn't wait to find out. "I wouldn't miss it for the world."

"Good," he said, actually rubbing his hands together. "Very good. Excellent, in fact. Oh — I'll want you to meet someone from DARDCO. It's conceivable that you'll be working with her to refine and publicize the cavity program."

"What — not with Williams?" Gail asked innocently.

Sloat smiled smugly. "Our Mr. Williams has a high opinion of his worth to DARDCO. And a quite inaccurate opinion, I might add. He's only a technician, after all. No, you'll be working with Miss Soto. Miss Alicia Soto. She's assistant to the Director of Research and Development. A most intriguing woman. And a very powerful one." He looked at Gail strangely, his eyes glittering. "You two will work well together. I know it. Now, if you'll excuse me, I have to get some telexes ready for Miss Liszt when she returns."

"Of course," Gail said. "I'll see you this evening."

"Eight o'clock," Sloat called. "In the meeting room."

"I'll be there," Gail assured him, deliberately echoing Williams' words. "You can count on it."

* * * * *

Back in her room, she stood under the shower, letting the warm water sluice over her, trying to make sense of the scene with Sloat. The man was hiding something. But if he had engineered the theft of her cavity location program, there was no way on this earth she could prove it. And what would ISAUR, or for that matter DARDCO, use it for anyhow? She couldn't imagine. Well, she supposed she would find out at the press conference.

Adjusting the water, she thought ruefully that at least she wouldn't have to dive any more. That suited her just fine. She poured shampoo into her palm and proceeded to wash her hair. She scrubbed, rinsed, and as the lather washed down her legs and back, she thought of Marike's softly stroking fingers. She leaned against the wall of the shower, suddenly weak. This was the first time she had permitted herself to think about the night before. Closing her eyes, the water drumming on her breasts, she felt again Marike's lips brushing her fingers, her lips, her nipples, her stomach, the soft skin of her inner thighs, alternately gentle and demanding, but always so sure. So vivid and recent was the memory that she found herself breathing faster as a moist heat grew between her thighs. And had the hot water not run out at that precise moment, Gail thought ruefully that she might have remained in the shower for another hour, lost in memory of what had been and anticipation of what was to come.

Smiling, she stepped out of the tub and wrapped herself in a towel. Padding out into the bedroom, she yawned, looking at her watch. Not even noon. She had plenty of time. She dried herself, then slipped naked between the sheets, setting her alarm. She intended to sleep for four hours, then call Marike and arrange to drive back to Osten's Bay to spend the night. But it would have to be after this silly press conference. Marike would understand. She yawned again, wondering what she would wear. Something simple. Not that she had much. Well, she'd worry about that later. Now, though she needed sleep, her thoughts returned to her night with Marike. It all *felt* right. But what was Marike thinking? Perhaps with her straightforward, uncomplicated nature, Marike lived only in the present. Gail wished she could be like that. She sighed. They had both been far too preoccupied last night to talk about the future. Would they have one — together? She would have to wait and see. Closing her eyes, she was instantly asleep.

130

Chapter 10

A door slammed someplace nearby, and Gail struggled awake, forcing her eyes open. Groggily, she reached for the clock. Ten minutes after seven! Why hadn't the alarm gone off? She saw in disgust that she had been so tired she had neglected to pull out the alarm pin. If it hadn't been for the door slamming, she might have slept right through the press conference. And now there was no time to telephone Marike. She'd just have to drive over to Osten's Bay after the press conference and arrive unannounced.

She got up. What on earth did one wear to a press conference? Sloat had told Williams to be sure and wear his tux, but the two of them would be in front of the television cameras. She hardly need worry about something like that, she thought bitterly. Resolutely telling herself to put all that out of her mind, she took white linen slacks and a long sleeve indigo silk blouse off the hangers and hastily dressed. Running a comb through her hair, she took a quick look at her sunburned nose and bleary eyes, and grimaced a little. She still looked as though she could use about twelve hours sleep.

On the path leading to the administration building, she spotted a familiar figure ambling along in the twilight, hands jammed into the pockets of cut-off jeans.

"Russ!" she called out, and the gangly redhead turned, smiling crookedly when he saw her.

"Hi," he said. "Say, did you hear the news?"

"I'm not sure," she told him. "I've heard some interesting things lately, though. You go first."

"Well, the diving's been canceled. Seems Sloat is getting a new toy for the cavity location program."

"Oh?" Gail asked. "What?"

Russ laughed. "A submersible. Can you believe it?"

Gail was past being amazed. "Maybe. Can I assume DARDCO is the donor?"

"Yup," Russ said. "Makes you wonder who we're working for here — science or DARDCO."

"I think I know the answer to that," Gail told him. "Say, if you're not doing anything, why don't you get dressed up and come to the press conference." She looked at her watch. "You've got just enough time. It's in the meeting room."

Russ cocked his head. "What's up?"

"Come and find out," Gail said. "Is it a date?"

Russ blushed furiously. "All right. I mean yes, I'd be happy to come. And thanks."

132

"There'll probably be a ton of food. Free drinks, too. These media types need a lot of sustenance. Seeing that you get some free goodies is the least I can do to thank you for all the help you've given me. And bring Toshio. See you in twenty minutes."

"Okay," Russ called over his shoulder, hurrying away. "And thanks again."

Twenty minutes. Just enough time to pay a visit to Marvin in the communications dome. Their earlier conversation had raised questions in her mind. She hoped he would be able to answer a few of them.

* * * * *

"I can't tell you that," Marvin said, pouring the last of a bottle of Scotch into a paper cup. "I've been sworn to silence," he told her melodramatically, gulping Scotch, swishing it around in his mouth, and finally swallowing. "God, that's awful," he gasped, shuddering.

"Why can't you tell me?" Gail asked him, impatient. "All I want to know is how this terrific breakthrough was made. Did Williams use the dive teams' data, or did he make some fundamental change in the program? And how did he know it was a breakthrough? Surely it has to be tested."

"Beats me," Marvin said, shaking his head. "My part in this earth-shaking scientific endeavor was small. Very small. Miniscule, in fact. But oh, so important. 'Ours not to reason why; ours but to do or die,' " he quoted, giggling.

Gail looked at her watch impatiently. She wasn't going to get anywhere with Marvin in the few minutes she had left before the press conference. Belching softly, he pillowed his head on his crossed arms and began to snore.

"Oh, hell," she said, and left him to it. After the press conference she'd come back, ply him with coffee, and walk him around a little. Maybe she could persuade him to make more sense then. Just what *had* his part been in the program breakthrough, anyway, she wondered. He had intimated to her in Sloat's office that it had been he, not Williams, who had the computer expertise. Williams didn't know RAM from ROM, Marvin had said. Had he been telling the truth? Or was it simply a case of sour grapes? And what exactly had Sloat's part been in this little operation, she wondered. That was the question that intrigued her most.

* * * * *

She met Russ just outside the door to the meeting room. He was dressed in a pair of khaki pants, a yellow short sleeved cotton shirt, and a red tie — evidently the best outfit he could find on such short notice. He looked awkward and ill at ease, surreptitiously fingering his tie, clearly uncomfortable with such formality.

"You're prompt," Gail told him. "Did Toshio decide not to come?"

"He's . . . sleeping," Russ said evasively.

Gail smiled. "Too much beer?"

Russ looked embarrassed. "How did you guess?"

"Oh, just lucky," she told him. It was amazing, but the rumors of the cavity location program's success seemed to have turned the entire Institute into a bunch of drunken sots. Were these indulgences really celebrations, she wondered, or were they expressions of relief? "Come on, let's hear what our leader has to say," she told Russ leading the way into the meeting room.

134

They elbowed through clumps of people, most of whom she didn't recognize, dodged the array of television cameral and cables clustered along one wall, and took a seat in the fourth row, well back from the places assigned to reporters.

"Wow, quite a production," Russ commented.

"Sure is," Gail agreed. "Well, Sloat claims he has an important announcement to make. You've heard about it, I presume? It seems half the Institute has."

Russ nodded. "The cavity location program? Yeah, Grant and Brian told us about it. Oh, by the way, Brian was looking for you the other night. I thought he wanted to apologize. I sent him up to your room, but I guess you'd already left for the Club Caribe."

"Mmmm," she replied. It was just as well that Brian hadn't found her. She'd have said some things she'd certainly have regretted.

"You know, I can't figure out what all this fanfare is about," Russ said.

"What?" Gail asked, only half paying attention.

"All this," Russ said. "I mean, I know the world's marine geologists will get pretty excited about the cavity location program. And I guess a few biologists will be interested, too. But why would DARDCO care? Or anyone else?" He pointed to a group of people standing at the front with Benjamin Sloat.

As Gail looked, one of the group — a strikingly attractive woman with café au lait skin, long, silky black hair, and smoldering dark eyes — turned and caught her glance. She was dressed in something clinging, something the color of dusky red wine, and the smile she gave Gail was clearly meant for her alone. Riveted, Gail found herself unable to look away. The woman was extraordinarily beautiful, with a primitive and exotic beauty Gail found breathtaking. As the woman continued to look directly at her, she felt her face grow hot. Then, thankfully, someone stepped between them, blocking the interchange. To her embarrassment, she found that Russ was still speaking to her, and that she hadn't heard a word he had been saying.

". . . deserve a press conference?" Russ wondered. "Sloat is telling the world about *this*?" He shook his head. "I must have missed something, but I sure can't figure out why."

"I expect we'll soon find out," Gail said absently, trying to peer between the milling figures for another glimpse of the raven-haired woman.

"Well, here we go," Russ said.

Sloat, Williams, and two other men filed up the steps and onto a slightly raised platform. But Gail's eyes were riveted on the figure that followed them up onto the platform — the dark-haired woman in the wine dress. Tall, slender, exotic, she moved with the grace of a jungle animal. She's Alicia Soto, Gail thought suddenly — DARDCO's assistant to the Director of Research and Development.

So mesmerized was she by the presence of the woman, she was totally unaware of anything else. The woman crossed her long legs, put her hands in her lap, and gazed indifferently out at the audience. Indifferently? No, haughtily, Gail thought. Yet her demeanor was not so much one of challenge or arrogance as it was one of immense self-confidence. This was a woman accustomed to wielding control, and from what Sloat had said, Alicia Soto was in control of much of DARDCO's research. If she was like most assistants, she held in her hands the power to make recommendations to her boss — in this case,

DARDCO's research and development director. As if aware of Gail's scrutiny, Alicia moved her head slightly, and her black hair rippled. She has a jaguar's beauty, Gail thought, and one must never forget that jaguars are predators. Untamed and dangerous.

Russ bent to speak to her, and she realized she hadn't heard a word of what Sloat had been saying. Twice now this woman had claimed her attention to the exclusion of everything else. "Now he's getting to it," Russ whispered. "Brother, what a long-winded introduction."

"The value of our new cavity location program cannot possibly be overestimated," Sloat said, reading from notes he held in one hand. He looked up, pausing for dramatic effect. "Far from being an esoteric scientific find, one with little practical application, it is, instead, a discovery with multi-billion dollar potential."

There was a buzz of excited voices. Sloat held up a hand for silence. "Yes, ladies and gentlemen, I said *billion*. Does this assertion sound fanciful?" He smiled benevolently at the audience. "Let me explain."

"It not only sounds fanciful, it sounds nuts," Russ whispered.

Gail found herself concentrating fiercely, a sinking sensation in her stomach. Multi-billion dollar potential? What on earth could he mean?

"When it came to the attention of our friends at DARDCO that the Institute was working on a cavity location program, they very generously offered to make available to us certain data they had accumulated. They provided us with some of their personnel and resources as well."

"Glib," Russ snorted. "Very glib. He's just described the death of independent inquiry, if anyone cared to read between the lines. What a guy. Our friends at DARDCO indeed."

But Gail hardly heard, so intently was she listening to Sloat. A terrible suspicion was blooming in her mind, and she had the overpowering feeling that in the next few minutes all her questions and misgivings about ISAUR would be answered. Her palms had begun to sweat; her heart was beating faster; she was having difficulty breathing.

Sloat continued. "So we can truly say that the breakthrough was a joint one. A perfect example of cooperation between science and industry. And now," he said, looking around smugly, "to the heart of the matter."

"Please," Russ begged.

"It's really very simple," Sloat said earnestly. "Cavities which occur in modern, living reefs are of interest primarily to scientists. But cavities which occur in ancient, dead reefs are of interest to every one of us." Television cameras whirred and reporters scribbled frantically while Sloat preened. "Or they should be. For these cavities contain oil. Think of it!" he exclaimed. "Finally, we have a tool for predicting where these cavities are likely to occur. A tool we can share with our nation's oil companies. Just think of the money they will save. At a minimum cost of one million dollars to sink a well, just imagine how their operations will change. Now they can spend their valuable dollars on exploration. On discovering new fields. On making this nation energy self-sufficient. No longer will we have to feel that our economy is chained to the policies of the Middle East, in thrall to the whims of desert sheiks. No! Soon, very soon, we will be free of all that. It's a mind-boggling proposition. Truly mind-boggling. It is, if I may be so bold as to say so, one of the most exciting developments of the modern age. And it was pioneered here, right here, at this modest facility, through cooperation between ISAUR and DARDCO." He looked around again, full of self satisfaction. "I'm sure you have questions," he told the reporters. "My secretary has prepared a press release that will help you with the technical data, and Dr. Williams here will be happy to answer questions on the computer program."

Suddenly Gail was unable to breathe. "I'm going out for some air," she told Russ.

Outside, in the cool night, she leaned against the wall of the building, filled with anger. It should have been Gail Murray up there answering questions about the computer program, not Williams. She was certain now that it was Williams — or perhaps Williams aided by Marvin — who had burgled her files to take a look at her program. Not pretty Charlie Henderson at Erindale. And she was sure that whatever had happened in the computer room last night, the electronic burglars now believed that they had access to the program and could copy or download it whenever they wished. Her program. She smiled grimly. Evidently they hadn't yet tried to run it. Presumably they had entered the computer with the codes she had supplied Miss Liszt, then cracked the college's file code, found her program, and simply taken a look to see that the program was there. Well, they were in for an enormous surprise: as soon as they ran the program, it would turn into nonsense.

She said a mental prayer of thanks to the grad student who had taught her about logic bombs. They were very useful devices — commands placed in the first line of a program, which, if not removed, instructed the program to self-destruct. Williams and Marvin would never be able to retrieve anything from the cavity location program.

She thought suddenly of the copy she had made, renaming it Research Expenses, and decided she'd better take additional steps to hide the file., It was, after all, the one remaining copy of the program. Was it really worth billions of dollars? She shook her head, wondering how she could have been so blind. Did it take a more diabolical mind than hers — the mind of a Benjamin Sloat — to see the practical applications of something like her program? Evidently.

She hurried through the dark to the communications dome, wondering what she was going to say to Marvin. Then she recalled that when she had paid him a visit just before noon, he had been well on the way to oblivion. Now it all made sense. His conscience had been bothering him! The theft of her program had driven him to drink, she thought wryly. Was it possible that one member of this burglary ring *had* a conscience? Perhaps Marvin could be appealed to. He might even be forced to admit the truth. She shook her head. More likely he would be passed out cold under one of the computer tables. Well, maybe that would be for the best. Her anger burned brightly as she thought of the theft, and she hoped for his sake that Marvin was incommunicado.

As she pushed open the door to the communications dome, loud snoring greeted her. Under different circumstances the situation might have been funny. She walked to the back of the dome. There on the floor, bottle cradled to his chest, lay Marvin. Her hands on her hips, she shook her head. She would just have to wait to ask her questions. The most important one — what role Benjamin Sloat had played in the theft of her program — burned in her brain.

She took a seat at one of the computer terminals and began the log-on procedure that would tie her with

Erindale's computer. She received the 701-C error message she expected. It meant that yet another unauthorized entry to her files had taken place. No further confirmation was needed.

And all signs pointed to one person as the mastermind of this operation — Benjamin Sloat. It was simply inconceivable that Marvin, or even Williams, had organized this thing alone. They would have needed information only Sloat possessed.

She was so angry her hands were shaking. Her contract here at ISAUR was all a sham. Sloat had hired her for only one reason — to get his hands on her program. How gullible she had been. She felt enraged, disappointed, and foolish in equal parts.

A thought occurred to her, a thought so chilling that her hands froze on the keyboard. Why had Sloat wanted her to work as divemaster if he truly had needed her program? Why would he have been willing to risk her having an underwater accident? Wasn't her brain more important to him than her diving skills? Surely he wouldn't have wanted to risk her, unless . . . She shivered. Unless by the time she arrived at ISAUR, Williams, Sloat's pet computer whiz, had already determined how to unlock her Erindale files and had taken a look at her program. Of course. That must have been the reason why Sloat was willing to have her dive. She had become dispensable. And the episode of the malfunctioning regulators — was she to still believe that was a practical joke? She shook her head in disbelief. But if not a joke, then what — attempted murder?

Hearing a noise behind her, she jumped, then looked over her shoulder. A printer had clattered to life, and she realized that it was the telex machine. She tried to will herself to relax. She needed to be calm for the job she was about to do. With a few keystrokes, she was about to access the only existing copy of a computer program worth untold millions of dollars. Her palms began to sweat, and she clenched her jaws together, concentrating.

The whole process turned out to be much easier than she had feared. And much quicker. She located the file in which she had hidden the cavity program and simply moved it from the Research Expenses file in the Gail Murray master dossier to a new master file which she created and named Marike. The cavity program she renamed Osten. Now even her colleagues at Erindale would be unable to gain access to the cavity program. In fact no one, unless he knew the name of the master file, would ever find the program. Williams and Marvin could search forever and never stumble upon it. She hesitated. What if something happened to her? Wouldn't she want someone else to have the program? Maybe. But who? After a moment's thought, she had the answer. Marike Osten.

It took only a moment to access a computer bulletin board in Toronto that she knew well, run by a pair of discreet hackers who would do almost anything for a price. She left a message on the board, with instructions that the hackers print it out and mail the hard copy to Marike's address in Bonaire.

"Cavity program in file Osten under Marike master file. Access codes are: Level one — Log onto Tymenet; dial (416) 555-1212, then Erindale Master Database: Faculty, then 77185; Level Two — GeolDeptFacResFiles; Level Three — Osten. That's it. The program is all yours to do with as you wish. My gift. Gail."

There. It was done. A roundabout way of ensuring that someone besides herself could gain access to the program, but, she thought, a safe way. Her hands shook as she logged off, and she sat at the terminal, brooding.

There was a noise behind her. The telex machine had clattered to a stop some minutes before. This new noise was something she could not identify.

"Hello, Dr. Murray," a quiet voice said.

She jumped. The voice belonged to Benjamin Sloat.

"Oh," she answered, trying not to seem as startled as she was. "Dr. Sloat. I, um, thought I'd just come in and do a little work."

"Commendable," he told her. "Most commendable."

To her surprise, his black bow tie was a bit askew and his eyes a trifle red. He also seemed to be breathing heavily, as if he had been running.

"I, too, am doing a little work. Besides telling the world about our marvelous discovery, that is. Look," he said, holding up a sheaf of papers. "Offers for the cavity program. We already have three oil companies bidding for it. What do you think of that?" He fixed her with his bloodshot eyes, smirking a little. "But then, you haven't told me what you thought of the press conference itself. Tell me, Dr. Murray. I'm eager to hear."

Gail regarded him cautiously. The man had more colors than a chameleon. Tonight he was belligerent and sarcastic — a far cry from the charming, agreeable director he liked to appear. She sensed that she ought to tread especially warily with him tonight. He seemed on the verge of something. A breakdown? Perhaps. Russ had told her how Sloat had changed over the past few months. Well, he certainly acted like a person shouldering an enormous load, a load which had gradually become too heavy. Now it seemed he was crumbling.

143

Gail looked at him impassively. She would not allow herself to feel sorry for him. This was the man who had masterminded the theft of her cavity program. She was convinced of it. Whatever trouble Benjamin Sloat found himself in, he richly deserved it. Let him stew.

"The press conference? I found it very interesting," she said.

Sloat snorted. "You're too nice, Dr. Murray. Far too nice." He looked down at her blearily. "You know, in the past few days I've been wondering about you. Just how nice are you prepared to be? You've survived a diving accident, your research career has gone up in electronic smoke, and still you're polite." He blinked his bloodshot eyes. "The long-suffering Dr. Murray. If I were you, I'd have run back to that college you came from. Why haven't you run, Dr. Murray? Why are you still here? And why are you still so nice?"

Gail stared at him, deliberately keeping any trace of emotion from her face. He was, she sensed, very close to coming apart at the seams. Strange. He didn't seem the type to have cold-bloodedly masterminded computer theft and attempted murder. Yet she supposed he had. Therefore he was capable of anything. And for the first time, she realized that Sloat had a point — why *was* she still here?"

"I have a contract," she told him. "ISAUR hired me to do a job."

"Go home, Dr. Murray," he said, swaying a little. "I'm releasing you from your contract." He shook his head. "Bringing you here was a mistake. Now be a very nice young lady and go away."

She opened her mouth to say something, but words seemed hollow. The truth was, she was genuinely frightened. If Sloat had come here tonight for the purpose

144

of frightening her out of her wits, he was succeeding. Clenching her fists so Sloat wouldn't see how her hands had begun to shake, she nodded. "Maybe I will. It does seem that you don't need me anymore."

Sloat chuckled. "Oh, I wouldn't say that. Let's just say that Toronto would be a much healthier place for you than Bonaire. Do you understand what I mean?" He swayed a little, and she realized with a start just how drunk he was. So that's what it took for him to come here and warn me, she thought, torn between pity for Sloat and fear for her own safety.

"I understand," she whispered. "And thank you."

"Don't thank me," he said roughly. "Just go. Run." He pressed one hand to the right side of his head and massaged his temple. "I have to go back now," he told her, stuffing the telexes inside his jacket. "People are waiting for these. I'm going to make them rich." He turned and began to walk unsteadily toward the door. She watched him go.

Lost in thought, Gail sat at the computer terminal for a few moments after Sloat's departure, then got up to go. Outside, the night was cool and dark, the sky sprinkled with stars. The shapes of palms made darker silhouettes against the charcoal sky, and a breeze from inland carried spicy, mysterious scents. She would just walk to the ocean and try to gather her thoughts. Standing on the beach and watching the waves was always therapeutic. And then she might even follow Sloat's advice. Leaving the Institute seemed a very appealing idea. But first she would have to call Marike and explain what had happened and why she was so late calling. Briefly she wondered if she shouldn't just leave — pack her things and drive to Osten's Bay. But how could she? She and Marike had spent only one night together. She could hardly expect her to welcome her with open arms. Having a lover and having a fugitive house guest were two different things.

A dark shape materialized in front of her, so close she was unable to avoid it. "Oof," she said, as she walked directly into whomever had been standing there in the dark. Someone definitely female, about Gail's height, and wearing a wonderfully seductive cologne — something reminiscent of dark, mossy places in the woods. Gail stepped back, the woman's hands on her arms. "I'm sorry," Gail apologized. "I didn't see you there."

"No, please," the woman said in a deep, husky voice. "It's I who should apologize. I came out here to escape all that noise and commotion at the party and I wasn't paying attention. It was I who stepped into *your* way. Please accept my apology."

"Thank you. I will," Gail said, her voice a little shaky.

Suddenly the events of the past few hours — the press conference, the steps she had taken to ensure the safety of the one remaining copy of the cavity program, her feelings of anger and betrayal, Sloat's warning — rose up and overwhelmed her. Before she knew what had happened, tears were running down her face and she was sobbing in the arms of this stranger.

"Sssh," the woman said, holding her and patting her back as one would a child. "It can't be all that bad."

Mortified, Gail struggled to regain her composure. How could she have just disintegrated at the first kind word this woman uttered? Was she so starved for compassion and understanding? She stepped back, disentangling herself from the woman's embrace. "I'm terribly sorry," she stammered. "I've had a rotten day, made even more rotten, if possible, by an unwelcome encounter with a drunk."

"Was the drunk our friend Benjamin Sloat, by any chance?" the woman asked.

"Yes, it was. But who are you?" Gail asked. "How did you know that?"

"I'm Alicia Soto," the woman answered. "I saw Sloat heading down the path to the communications dome and figured he might be after you. Why don't we continue this conversation somewhere else?" Alicia said. "I imagine you have some questions you'd like to ask me. I certainly have some I'd like to ask you."

"What kind of questions?" Gail asked warily.

"Dr. Murray, I don't believe for a moment that Williams and Sloat came up with that cavity location program between them. Williams does write software for DARDCO, but he's about as creative as a jellyfish. And Sloat, well, what he knows about computers could be written on the head of a pin. It's inconceivable that those bumblers could have written such a sophisticated program. Do I make myself clear?"

Gail tried not to let her surprise show. Was this woman really going to turn out to be an ally? She seemed to have neither respect nor liking for Williams. Or for Sloat. But what did Alicia want with her? She decided that it might be worth the time to try to find out. "I don't understand what this has to do with me," she said evasively.

"Please, Dr. Murray. I've read your research papers. I know perfectly well that you wrote that program. What I want to know is how Sloat and Williams got hold of it. And what they promised you."

Gail thought furiously. If Alicia Soto was going to be an ally, she would have to be pretty specific about what DARDCO had to offer. And she would have to convince

Gail that she had known nothing about the attempted theft of the cavity program. "Have you had a chance to examine the program?" she asked nonchalantly.

"Not yet," Alicia said. "Williams only informed me this morning that the program existed. I do believe, however, that it can do what Sloat and Williams say it can. Williams may be a plodder, but he's a very careful plodder." Alicia was silent for a moment. "How did they entice you to give them the program, Dr. Murray?"

Gail closed her eyes. Could she trust Alicia? After all, she worked for DARDCO. But what harm would it do to tell the truth? It seemed as thought Alicia really didn't know that the program had been stolen. "They didn't entice me," she said flatly. "They stole it."

Alicia gasped. "Stole it? But how? My God, this is terrible!" She grasped Gail's arm. "We have to talk. Is there someplace we can go? Someplace where we won't be disturbed?"

Gail thought about Russ, waiting for her at the party, about the phone call she had to make to Marike — she needed to talk to each of them. But she really did want to hear what Alicia had to say. Perhaps there would be a chance to salvage something from this mess. "We could go to my room," she said.

* * * * *

It's astounding," Alicia said, kicking off her shoes and reclining on Gail's bed, one leg drawn up under her. She brushed her black hair off her shoulders and leaned back against the headboard, carefully balancing her glass of Scotch on one knee. "From what you've told me, Sloat and Williams are simply burglars. How on earth did they think they'd get away with it?" She shook her head in

148

disgust, sipping her drink. "DARDCO certainly wants a cavity location program, but this isn't the way we want to acquire it. I wouldn't mind another one of these," she said, holding out her glass. "Excellent Scotch, incidentally."

Gail rose quickly from the chair by the window and refilled Alicia's glass. She tried to hide her concern. Since Alicia's arrival in her room almost half an hour ago, the woman had talked in generalities, reiterating only what Gail already knew. Oh, she was properly sympathetic, but when was Alicia going to get to the point? She wanted to call Marike. To do so she would have to go to the administration building or the cafeteria — they had the only public phones in the Institute. She stole a glance at her watch — almost ten o'clock.

"Oh!" Alicia said, as Scotch slopped over the rim of her glass onto her dress. She jumped up.

"Wait here. I'll get a towel from the bathroom," Gail said. She hurried back to find Alicia had slipped out of her dress and was holding it up critically, examining the spot. But it wasn't the dress that kept Gail immobile in the middle of the room. It was Alicia herself. Underneath the dress, she'd worn only a pair of brief black panties. Her café au lait skin glowed like bronze in the lamplight, and as she turned, reaching for the towel, Gail saw what a beautiful body she had. Her breasts were small, high and firm, the nipples rosy and erect, her stomach was flat and smooth, and her long legs were trim and taut. Gail swallowed, trying not to stare as she handed Alicia the towel.

"I think the spot will come out," Alicia said, dabbing at it. "It's no great loss if it doesn't. I'll just hang it in the bathroom to dry. Oh, I topped off both our drinks — yours is on the dresser." Turning, she walked to the bathroom.

149

Gail moved like an automaton to the dresser, Alicia's almost naked body fresh in her mind, and reached for the drink. Taking a healthy swallow, she grimaced. Perhaps she should give up drinking. It tasted awfully bitter tonight. At that moment, Alicia returned from the bathroom, and Gail was unable to think about anything else.

Alicia stood for a moment in the bathroom door, looking inscrutably at Gail. "I've got something you could put on," Gail offered. "A robe. Or perhaps you'd like —"

"No," Alicia said, walking slowly toward Gail, a tight smile on her face. "I'm fine the way I am."

"All right," Gail said, feeling foolish and gauche. She turned to sit at the room's little table again. A wave of dizziness overcame her. She had one hand on the chair, so she was able simply to collapse in it. She shook her head in perplexity, trying to clear her fuzzy thoughts.

"What's wrong?" Alicia said, kneeling beside her.

"I'm not sure," Gail said. "I felt a little dizzy for a moment. I think it will pass."

"I wouldn't worry about it," Alicia said, rising to one knee. "You've had a difficult day. Why don't you come and lie on the bed?"

The idea seemed very appealing. "I think I will," she said. She clutched the arms of the chair and tried to stand but found to her dismay that her legs wouldn't obey her. What on earth is the matter with me, she wondered.

"Let me help," Alicia said, putting an arm around Gail's shoulders.

Gail staggered to the bed, and as she lay down she realized that something was terribly wrong. The room had begun to ripple disconcertingly, and she was having enormous difficulty concentrating her thoughts. She closed her eyes, wondering if she was drunk. No, she wasn't. She hadn't had nearly enough to drink. So she must be sick. Maybe some tropical disease.

She closed her eyes and felt like a swimmer being sucked slowly, inexorably, down into a viscous, black whirlpool. She tried to move her arms and legs but felt as though she were struggling in molasses.

How long she struggled she had no memory — it could have been a minute, or an eon. But when at last she opened her eyes, it was to a totally confusing scene.

Where was she? More important, who was she? Looking down, she realized that she was a woman, naked, on a bed in an unfamiliar room. And beside her on the bed lay another naked woman, one whose raven hair fanned out over the pillow. The woman looked at her with eyes like chips of obsidian, and raised her hand to touch Gail's face.

"Hello," she said.

"Hello," Gail responded automatically, waiting for all this to make sense.

"Do you know where you are?"

"No," Gail said.

"You're here in your room. You haven't been . . . well. People have been trying to take advantage of you. But you're safe with me. I'm your friend." The woman's hand stroked Gail's throat, pinching the soft skin gently. "It's all right if none of this makes sense now. It will soon. So you won't worry, will you?"

"No," Gail answered, eager to please this woman who promised that everything would soon make sense, and that she would be safe. "I won't worry."

"Good," the woman said, her hand around Gail's throat. "Very good. All you have to worry about is pleasing me. Now, I want to ask you a few questions. And you will want to answer them, won't you?"

151

"Yes," Gail assured her. "I will." And there was no doubt in her mind that she would. She had no clear idea of who this woman was, how either of them had gotten here, or even where here was. All she knew was that she wanted to please this woman who was her friend.

"*Very* good," the woman said. She began to stroke Gail's breasts, her long sensitive fingers lingering over the nipples. Gail murmured in pleasure. "Oh, you like that," the woman said softly. "I rather thought you would. And you don't want to say anything that will make me stop what I'm doing, now do you?"

"Oh no," Gail replied, closing her eyes.

"All right," the woman said, "let's begin with something easy. Do you remember your name? And what you do for a living?"

Gail thought. "Yes," she said finally. "I'm Gail Murray. I'm a marine geologist. I work at ISAUR."

"Excellent," the woman said, running her nails over Gail's breasts. Gail shivered under her touch. "Now, can you tell me why you came to ISAUR?"

That was easy, Gail thought. "To help Dr. Sloat perfect the Institute's cavity location program."

"Of course," the woman said, pinching Gail's nipples between her fingers, the sudden pain almost pleasurable. "Very good. Now, tell me something: did you download your cavity program onto the Institute's computer?"

"Yes," Gail replied, doing her best to ignore a little voice nagging in the back of her mind, urging her not to answer. Why shouldn't she answer? This woman was her friend. Besides, it was becoming increasingly difficult to concentrate on anything but the woman's hands on her breasts. And when one hand moved lower, to stroke the smooth skin of Gail's stomach, she began to tremble.

152

"Good, good," the woman crooned. "Now think, Gail: what did you do to the cavity program? You scrambled it somehow. Oh, it was very clever of you, but I want to unscramble it. Can you tell me what you did?"

"I put a logic bomb in the program," Gail replied unhesitatingly. "The first time the program's run, it disintegrates into gibberish. It can't be unscrambled."

"Oh dear," the woman said. "That was very naughty of you. But it's not irretrievable, is it? Why, a clever young lady like you could just download the program all over again, now couldn't she?"

"No," Gail replied. "It can't be downloaded now." The woman's hand strayed between Gail's legs, brushing the insides of her thighs, tantalizing her. Gail moaned.

"We have all night," the woman told her. "If you give me the right answers, I might do something more than just touching. Would you like that?"

"Yes," Gail replied, ignoring the voice in her mind yammering caution. "I'd like that very much."

"All right," the woman said. "Now tell me why the program can't be downloaded."

Gail tried her best to think. But it was so hard. The woman's hand on her thighs had gently parted her pubic hair, and one finger had begun an agonizingly delicious stroking. Moaning, she clutched the bedspread.

"Tell me," the woman urged, moving her finger just a little and bending to take one of Gail's nipples in her teeth. Gail gasped in pleasure. "Tell me why the program can't be downloaded."

Gail remembered it now. "I hid it," she answered, her voice shaking. "It's in another file."

"How clever of you," the woman said. She raised her head from Gail's breast. "You're really doing very well," she told Gail, her dark eyes enormous in the lamplight.

"Very well. I think I'll reward you a little. And myself, too."

She rose to her knees and straddled Gail's legs. As she bent over Gail, her black hair cascaded over Gail's body like a ebony silken curtain. Gail wanted to raise a hand to touch it, but her arms felt like lead. Raising even a hand was impossible. She closed her eyes. Now the woman was kissing Gail's nipples, taking first one, then the other, in her teeth, biting just a little — not enough to cause pain but enough to cause a familiar hot aching to begin between Gail's thighs. The woman's mouth moved lower, nibbling and biting the flesh of Gail's stomach. Repositioning herself, she knelt between Gail's knees.

"Bend your legs," she said, her voice sounding strangely choked. Gail was only too eager to obey and found to her surprise that when she willed her knees to bend, they did. Nor did they feel like lead any more. However, her mind was unable to concentrate on these things because the woman had bent to kiss her thighs.

Then she felt herself stroked by two hands — hands that moved from her inner thighs to meet in the now damp hair between her legs. She felt the woman's deft fingers stroke only a moment longer, finally coming to the small hard bud she sought. "Yes," the woman said. "Yes." When she knelt to take the sensitive bud between her lips, Gail cried out, so exquisite was the sensation. And when the woman opened her mouth, touching Gail with her tongue, Gail reached down and clutched the woman's hair. My arms, Gail thought, I can move my arms!

Then two things happened at once. The woman raised her head to look at Gail in astonishment and, outside in the hall, someone began a furious pounding on Gail's door.

154

"I can see that you're in there — your light's on," an angry voice called from the other side of the door. "So let me in, dammit!"

Gail tried to sit up, but the woman pushed her back. Whose voice was that? She could almost say the name. In the recesses of her memory recognition stirred and, with it, awareness that this woman in her bed was a total stranger. Like water through an open floodgate, her memory returned in a rush: this woman was Alicia Soto, DARDCO's assistant to the Director of Research. And they were by no means friends. The content of Alicia's recent interrogation came back to her and with it a horrible realization: Alicia and Sloat were co-conspirators! Had it been from Alicia that Sloat had warned her to flee?

Gail shook her head to clear it. It was as though she had been under a spell, a magic spell, one that had made her forget and obey, one that had made her compliant, totally subservient to Alicia. Only it hadn't been a magic spell at all, she realized, but a chemical spell instead. Alicia Soto had drugged her!

"You put something in my drink," Gail said indignantly.

The other woman smiled and reached down beside the bed. When she brought her hand up, it held a short barrelled revolver. "I didn't want to have to use this," she said. "I preferred the other way. But . . ." she shrugged. "Pay attention, Miss Murray. This is a .38 caliber revolver. It's not a woman's gun, and it's certainly not a toy. If you look closely, you'll see it's loaded." She wrapped one of the pillows around the hand holding the gun. "The noise will be loud, but not too loud. Only the person outside that door will hear it. And then I'll have to use the gun on her, too." She smiled tightly. "So send whoever is in the hall away."

Gail looked at the door longingly, then back at the gun.

"Come off it, Gail!" the voice called from the hall. "You can't hide in there forever. I thought we got all this settled last night! Now open the bloody door!" The pounding began again.

It was Marike! But how could she communicate anything to her without putting her life in danger? Gail closed her eyes. "Go . . . go away," she called out.

"Louder," Alicia urged. "Much louder. And sound as though you mean it."

"Go away!" Gail shouted, in tears by now. "Just go away!"

The pounding stopped. "Gail, I can't believe you're saying this," Marike exclaimed. "Why don't you let me in. We'll talk." The doorknob rattled.

"No!" Gail yelled. "Leave me alone!"

Silence. Then, in a voice so quiet Gail scarcely heard it, Marike answered her. "All right, I will. I've come after you twice, Gail Murray. I won't do it again. As far as I'm concerned, this is it. The end." Neither the pounding nor the shouting resumed. Marike was gone.

"Well, well," Alicia said, a little smile on her face. "It seems as though your love life isn't going at all well. Who was that?"

Gail set her lips in a grim line. Now that she had command of her faculties, she had no intention of telling this woman anything. "Go to hell," she said.

"Goodness, such language," Alicia commented. She crossed the room to her purse and clothes, which were on one of the chairs. Alicia tossed the pillow to the floor and put the gun down on the table. "Don't do anything foolish," she warned. From her purse she withdrew a slim plastic case, no larger than a fountain pen. The gun in one hand, the plastic case in the other, she came toward Gail.

"Lie back down on the bed," Alicia commanded. Gail couldn't see that she had any choice but to obey. "Take this," Alicia said, handing Gail the plastic case. "Remove the top." Gail briefly debated throwing the case across the room, but fear held her back. Two slim syringes, each filled with clear liquid and labelled with strips of colored tape, lay inside the case. "Give me the one marked with red tape," Alicia said. "And put the case on the bedside table." Gail did as she was told.

"Now," Alicia told her, "you're going to sleep for a while. In a few hours, once we've had a chance to hunt in Erindale's computer files for that program of yours, we'll be back. Oh, we'll find it, never fear. And you won't fool us twice with that logic bomb trick of yours, as clever as it was. No. This time you'll remove the bomb before we run the program."

Gail's heart sank. Sloat, Williams, and Alicia would be able to make her do it, too. "Give me your arm," Alicia said, depressing the plunger of the syringe and clearing the air from it in a spurt of liquid. "No tricks now."

Tricks? Gail hesitated, trying desperately to think of one.

Alicia's eyes became angry slits. "Your arm!" she hissed.

Defeated, Gail held her arm out.

"Make a fist," Alicia said. With a practiced jab, she plunged in the needle. "There," she said, smirking in satisfaction. Gail wondered briefly how she could ever have thought her beautiful. "That should keep you for a while," Alicia said. She walked to the table and began to dress. "I'll see you later," she said. "I hope you're going to be cooperative when you wake up. Although if you aren't ..."

Gail opened her mouth to tell Alicia just where she could go and what she could do, but a wave of weakness washed over her and she lost consciousness.

Chapter 11

Gail fought her way up out of sleep, feeling as though she were swimming through mud. Some nameless urgency propelled her, and she struggled upward toward consciousness. Finally, she was able to take a precarious grip on reality and opened her eyes. Forcing herself, she sat up and swung her legs out of bed. Then, to her relief, she remembered everything. Improbably, the room looked exactly the same, and she wondered how it could after so much had happened. Her head ached fiercely and her legs wobbled, but otherwise she felt surprisingly all right. What time was it? Just past three a.m. She recalled looking at her watch just before Alicia had given her that shot, and the time then had been just after one.

Staggering to the bathroom, she splashed water on her face and wondered briefly what had gone wrong. Shouldn't she still be out cold, waiting for Alicia's and Sloat's arrival? Alicia must have miscalculated the dosage. Well, if her luck held for one more minute, she'd be out of here. She found some shorts and a T-shirt and pulled them on as fast as she could. Jamming her feet into her old Reeboks, she grabbed her wallet and ran from the room.

On the first floor, she hurried down the hall to Russ and Toshio's room. Knocking softly first, she opened the door and went in.

"Russ," she called urgently, flipping on the light switch and shaking him. "Wake up! I need the keys to the jeep."

"Mmph," he muttered, sitting up and looking at her dazedly, his red hair standing on end. "You need what?"

"The keys to the jeep. And for God's sake, don't tell anyone you saw me."

"What's going on?" he asked, rubbing his eyes and sitting up. "Are you all right?"

"No," she told him. "That's why I'm running away. Sloat and Alicia Soto will be after me soon. They haven't yet gotten their hands on my cavity program, and I don't think they'll stop trying." Halfway to the door a thought occurred to her. "If I were you two, I might disappear, too. Sloat knows we're friends. He might think I've confided something about the program to you."

Toshio's head emerged from his bed's covers. "I agree," he said to Russ. "Why don't we go and pay your caterer friend a little visit? She did seem most eager to have you spend the night."

"Yeah," Russ said to Toshio. "That's not a bad idea."

Then he turned back to Gail. "But how will we get in touch with each other if we're all hiding?"

"I'll call the hotel. What's your friend's name?"

"It's Zoe," Russ said, scrubbing one hand through his hair. "I know you can't tell me where you're going, but you will be careful, won't you? And you will get in touch with us?"

"You can count on it," Gail told him, closing the door quietly behind her.

* * * * *

From the shelter of a clump of palm trees, she looked out over the parking lot. Everything seemed normal. Taking a deep breath, she ran for the jeep, feeling as though a hundred eyes were on her. As she started the engine, she recalled the gun in Alicia's hand. No, I didn't imagine all this, she told herself as she wheeled out of the parking lot and onto the gravel road to the main gates. Incredible as it seemed, it had all really happened.

Damn Alicia Soto anyway, Gail thought savagely. She knew now who the mastermind of this whole operation had been. So Alicia had read her research papers, had she? Gail wondered how long that power-hungry witch had been planning things. She had first heard from Sloat in March, so that meant the duo had been hatching this plot for at least six months. Probably longer.

The coast road was deserted at this hour of the morning. She put the jeep in fourth gear, put her foot to the floor, and drove like a madwoman toward Osten's Bay.

* * * * *

She saw the other jeep at about the same time its

161

driver saw her. Against the rising sun, it looked like one of the Institute jeeps. She changed lanes, set her jaw, and drove straight at it. It began honking its horn but she ignored it. At the last minute, it swerved off the road and she passed it in a swirl of dust. She smiled triumphantly and moved back over to her side of the road. Had she bought herself some time? She certainly hoped so. On the next hill, however, she knew she was wrong.

The jeep, which she could now plainly see was blue, came up the hill behind her like a rocket. "Damn!" she shouted, and put her foot down. But the balky Institute jeep refused to go any faster. Inexorably, the gap narrowed between her and the blue jeep. Five hundred feet, two hundred, one hundred . . . Now it was right behind her. She twitched the steering wheel to the left and moved over to block its path, determined not to let it get ahead of her. The two vehicles crested the hill, and the blue jeep pulled up beside her on the right. She was about to pull the wheel back toward it in an attempt to force it off the road again when she saw the driver. It was Marike!

Gail braked. The blue jeep shot ahead. Marike drove off the road, jumped out of the jeep, and ran back shouting. "You maniac! What were you trying to do — kill me?"

Gail looked anxiously back down the road toward the Institute. "I was trying to lose you. I didn't know it was you. I thought it was someone from the Institute."

Marike glared. "From the Institute? Why — what's wrong?"

"I can't explain now," Gail said. "I just have to get away from there."

"I don't know why I bothered to come back for you — intuition, I guess. I knew something was wrong when I stood there outside your room making a fool of myself. I

162

just knew it."

"Yes, you're right," Gail said, again glancing down the road. "I'm in a whole lot of trouble. I need a safe place to hide from Benjamin Sloat. And from his crony Alicia Soto of DARDCO. But I don't think we should discuss it here."

"All right," Marike said. "You'd better get in my jeep. Drive yours back into the brush over there. With luck, no one will see it."

Gail hid the Institute jeep as well as she could and came running back. Marike's tires screamed on the asphalt as the little jeep jumped ahead, and Gail hung on as they sped off down the road.

"We could take a roundabout route," Marike explained, "but the coast road to Osten's Bay is a lot faster. If we're lucky, we'll get there first, and I'll just close the road. Then no one can get in. We'll call Rolf Klee, and that will be that."

Gail nodded, but privately she wasn't so sure. Would a closed road stop Sloat and Alicia? She didn't think so. And Rolf Klee was only one man. Besides, what could Sloat and Alicia be accused of? Gail had no proof for any of her claims. No, they needed a better plan. But first, she would settle for getting to Osten's Bay.

Gail saw the helicopter before Marike did. She would have heard it long before she saw it, but the roar of the wind past the open jeep made hearing almost impossible. The bright orange helicopter, bearing DARDCO's letters and logo, swooped over the jeep from behind and hovered over the road at a height of ten feet perhaps thirty yards ahead.

"Shit!" Marike yelled. With instants to make a decision, Marike did what Gail herself would have done. She kept driving. At the last possible moment, the

163

helicopter rose into the air, and the jeep sped underneath it.

Gail looked back over her shoulder. The helicopter was making a giant circle about a hundred yards behind them. "It's no good, Marike," she said in dismay. "They can try that as many times as they need to. Eventually they'll force us to stop."

"I know," Marike said, braking for a particularly sharp turn. "And the road coming up is too dangerous to drive like this. We're almost at Karpata. Dammit, anyhow! Fifteen more minutes and we'd have been safe. Why do they want you, anyhow?"

Gail gripped the sides of the seat. "I prevented them from stealing something of mine."

"The cavity program!" Marike yelled. "I heard it on the news. That's why I stormed over to have it out with you. I figured you'd helped them make this great breakthrough."

"Under other circumstances, I might have," Gail told her. "That's what I was hired to do. But I didn't get the chance. They stole my program. Or at least they thought they'd stolen it. I sabotaged it to protect it. But I hid another copy. They know that. That's why they're after me."

"Ha!" Marike yelled. "Good for you! Well, what we have to do is get you away from this bloody helicopter and everything will be all right. Damn!" she said, taking the next corner on two wheels. Gail looked across Marike at the left side of the road. They were at the Karpata bluffs. The blue ocean dashed itself in foamy breakers against the rocks at the base of the cliff. She remembered this part of the drive from her trip to Osten's Bay. It had intimidated her then. Now, going sixty miles an hour around these blind curves, a helicopter pursuing them, it terrified her.

Like an angry hawk, the helicopter swooped ahead of them, rose to gain height, hovered for an instant, then dived straight at them.

"That guy is crazy!" Marike screamed. "He's going to kill us!" Gail could see the desperation on her face as she fought the wheel, sending the jeep into a screaming slide as they cornered. Gail felt the jeep lose the struggle an instant before Marike cried out. It drifted toward the left side of the road despite everything Marike did. "We're going over the edge!" Marike yelled. "The water's deep here. Jump when I tell you!"

It was almost beautiful, Gail recalled later. Time seemed to slow as the jeep sideslipped toward the edge of the cliff. Then they were in the air, flying free. Was this a dream? She glimpsed turquoise water studded with reefs fifty feet below as the jeep's nose began to dip, and she could feel them falling.

Then Marike yelled. "Jump! Now!"

Gail looked down, hesitating, and Marike pushed her. She fell out the open door of the jeep and had the uncanny experience of seeing the jeep suspended in the air beside her before she hit the water. Then she knew it was no dream.

The cold and the force of the fall drove the breath from her body. Blinded by a flurry of bubbles, choking, disoriented, she flailed about, trying to find her way to the surface. Finally she saw what she took to be the sun — a round pewter disc gleaming through a blizzard of bubbles in an indigo sky. Willing herself not to cough, she kicked frantically for the sun.

An instant before she would have blacked out, her head broke the surface, and she crawled up onto a lump of coral, heedless of the cuts she was receiving. Sobbing, she coughed and choked, finally retching up the seawater she had swallowed. Then, when she was able, she looked around for Marike. There were only the round pale shapes of brain coral poking above the surface of the blue water. Marike was nowhere to be seen.

An angry buzzing came from the sky, and she submerged quickly, taking shelter under an outgrowth of coral. The helicopter circled, and she watched it warily. Finally, it made one low pass over the water then disappeared to the north in the direction of the Institute. She knew in her bones that the searchers would be back.

"Hi," a voice called from behind her.

"Marike!" She turned. There, between two brain coral heads, Marike had wedged herself. She was bleeding freely from a cut above her eyebrow, and her arms and hands were covered with coral cuts, all bleeding alarmingly. "Are you —"

"All right?" Marike shook her head. "I'm afraid not." She raised one arm to brush the blood out of her eyes, and Gail could see that her hand was shaking. "I think I've broken my leg. I got tangled up in the steering wheel and whacked my head on the door frame when we hit the water. I'm having a little trouble seeing straight," she said, laughing shakily. "I'm afraid this is it for me."

"What do you mean?" Gail asked in horror.

"Leave me here," Marike said. "They want you, not me. There's no reason for them to do me any harm. They'll be back here as soon as they can get a boat. An hour at the outside. I'll be all right until then. It shouldn't take you more than half that time to swim to Osten's Bay. Then you can call Rolf to storm the Institute and set me free." She giggled a little. "He'd like that."

"Tough talk," Gail said, swimming to her side. "You'll just sit here on the coral for an hour with a

166

concussion and a broken leg, waiting for help, right?"

"Something like that," Marike said, closing her eyes. Her face turned deathly pale, and before Gail could do anything, Marike simply slipped beneath the surface.

"No!" Gail shouted, and immediately reached under the water for the bright tangle of Marike's hair. Holding her head above the water, she hauled Marike's shoulders up onto a small brain coral, and scrambled up beside her. Marike lay face down, scarcely breathing. In a moment, however, she groaned, and moved her head.

"Jesus," she said. "Everything just got . . . far away. Did I pass out?"

"Yes, you did," Gail said, feeling panicked. How much time did they have before she saw one of the Institute's sleek motorboats on the horizon? Much less than an hour now, she guessed. And leaving Marike here was completely out of the question. She didn't share Marike's confidence that the Institute people wouldn't harm her. And who was to say that Marike wouldn't lose consciousness again before help arrived, and slip beneath the surface of the ocean to drown? "Listen," she told Marike with far greater confidence than she felt. "I'm going to get us out of here."

"Oh?" Marike said, biting her lip against the pain. "How?"

"Easy," Gail said. "It will be just like lifesaving class. You'll be the drowning victim, and I'll be the rescuer. I'm going to tow you. All you have to do is lie on your back and look at the sky."

Marike looked at Gail, hope in her eyes. "Do you think you can swim that far?" she whispered. "I'll be dead weight. The best I can do is just try to keep afloat."

"I can swim that far," Gail said, forcing a smile. "Don't worry about me."

"All right," Marike said, tears running down her face. "I'm sorry," she apologized. "Let's try it."

The sight of Marike's tears aroused in Gail a fierce protectiveness, all the more amazing because she had never felt anything remotely like it before. "I love you, Marike Osten, and I sure don't intend to lose you now. Besides," she added lightly, "I was the lifesaving champion of my class. I've even got a medal to prove it. So come on — let's get you nice and comfortable. We've got a swim to make."

*****

The muscles in Gail's shoulders screamed at her to stop; her legs felt like rubber and the salt water blinded her every time she put her head down into a wave. And just as Marike had warned, she was dead weight. For the first hour or so, Gail tried to talk to Marike, to keep her friend alert, but finally she had to give up and save her breath for swimming. The sea had grown steadily rougher over the past hour, and she found she was swimming up the side of each wave and falling down into its trough.

She was towing Marike with a harness she had made from her own T-shirt ripped into strips and tied under the other woman's arms. It was an awkward arrangement, but it worked. Marike did her best to keep her head up out of the water, and for a long time she answered Gail gamely, but at last, she, too, fell silent. Finally it seemed to Gail that there was no other world than this body she was trapped in — a body whose muscles burned as if afire and whose brain had long ago ceased to function. She had even stopped looking at the horizon. There was only the drag of Marike behind her, the sight of her own hand cutting through the choppy blue water, the taste of salt on her mouth, and the sobbing of her own breath in her ears.

And at last the moment she had been dreading arrived, the moment when she was unable to swim another stroke. Weeping with agony and frustration, she simply stopped swimming. A wave nudged Marike's body against her, and she turned in the water to look into her friend's eyes, to apologize, to say something meaningful before the sea took them both under. She put her arms around Marike and kissed her, treading water with the last of her strength. "I'm sorry," she said.

"But we're here," Marike said, coughing a little as a wave broke over her head, trying gamely to keep afloat. "You did it."

Gail looked around. There was only open water. "No, Marike. I didn't."

"Look behind you," Marike whispered.

Feebly, Gail looked over her shoulder. A beach — and the pilings of a dock! But she knew she could never swim to that beach. It might as well be on the moon. However, just before she despaired completely, before she called out to God at the unfairness of it all, she felt herself seized by some elemental force. A wave gripped them both and lifted them, propelling them toward the shore. It felt as if they were in the grip of a giant's hand, a hand that Providence had decided would reach down to deliver them from their agony. The hand pushed them toward the beach, and just when Gail was certain it would dash them to bits on the shore, it released them, and they tumbled out of the surf and onto the sand. In disbelief, she clutched handfuls of wet, gritty sand and pressed her cheek into the beach. Then she wept in earnest — great racking sobs, sobs of incredulity, of gratitude, of humility. They were safe.

169

Chapter 12

"It's not good enough!" Marike said, throwing across the room the pencil she had been using to try to scratch inside her cast. She sat at her desk in the living room at Osten's Bay, Gail in an easy chair opposite her. "You can't hide here until Sloat and DARDCO give up looking for you. Dammit, you have your life to get on with." Seeing Gail's expression, she threw up her hands. "I know, I know. It's *your* life. Not mine. But you know as well as I do that hiding isn't the answer."

Gail looked away from Marike, out the window at the peaceful afternoon scene at Osten's Bay. A dive boat was just pulling in, depositing a load of happy, tired SCUBA divers. Toshio and Russ made excellent divemasters, she thought. Marike had provided them with room and board, and well-paid jobs. And Thomas, Marike's workman, equipped with his new two-way radio, made an extremely diligent lookout. Young Thomas' new duties included completely rebuilding the rock wall at the edge of the property adjoining the coast road — a locale from which he was in a position to inspect all visitors to Osten's Bay. Twice in two days he had radioed ahead to warn Gail and Marike that DARDCO's "filthy spies" were on the property.

Marike was right about not being able to hide forever. After only three days of this, Gail was thoroughly sick of it. And running away certainly wasn't the answer. Sloat could find her easily if she went to another college. But what *was* she to do? Give up marine geology altogether? Change her name? Go into hiding? Where? She sighed. No reasonable answer occurred to her.

"What choices do I have?" Gail asked wearily. "Sloat and Alicia won't go away just because I want them to. They're determined to have that program. They're probably in hot water for letting the program, and me, get away. I'll bet they're turning the island upside down looking for me."

Marike snorted. "Let them stew." She was tapping her fingers on the desk top. "You know," she said thoughtfully, "I have an idea. I can't make them stop looking for you, but maybe I can figure out a way to heat up the hot water they're in." Her eyes sparkled with excitement. "It would accomplish the same thing. They'd go away."

"What do you have in mind?" Gail wanted to know. "I don't see what we can possibly do to them. Rolf can't even

171

think of a crime they've committed, except maybe speeding on the coast road."

"Just wait a minute," Marike said. "Let me show you something." She rummaged around in the pile of papers on her desk, then withdrew a copy of *The Wall Street Journal*. Thumbing through it rapidly, she finally found what she was looking for, folded the paper, and gave it to Gail. "Look at the story on page four," Marike said. "Read the headline."

"DARDCO's Stock Soars 27 Points on Rumors of Cavity Location Device," Gail read. "Well, it's hardly a device — it's a technique," she quibbled. "And I don't see what it has to do with us. So, DARDCO stockholders are getting rich. So what?"

Marike smiled. "In all the excitement of making such huge profits, don't you think that Sloat and Alicia's boss, whoever he or she is, might just be overlooking the fact that the program hasn't been delivered yet?"

Gail was skeptical. "Maybe."

"And that twenty-seven point advance was just yesterday's increase," Marike pointed out. "The stock rose thirty-three points the day before and opened trading today with orders stacked up to the sky. It's hot, Gail. Everyone is jumping on DARDCO's bandwagon."

"So how does this help us?" Gail asked again.

"We reverse the process," Marike said triumphantly. "We make the stock go down."

Gail shook her head. Was Marike joking? "Marike, come on. Even if we *could* make the stock go down," she said skeptically, "and I doubt that we could, what would that do for us except give us the satisfaction of seeing DARDCO bigwigs — and a lot of little shareholders — lose a lot of money?"

"What it would do for us," Marike said emphatically, "is exactly what you need done — it would get Sloat and Alicia off your back. Don't you think their boss, once he — and the company — starts to lose money, is going to blame it on Sloat and Alicia? Especially if the cavity program is, say, rumored to be a hoax?"

Gail frowned. "It's not a hoax, of course. It really does exist."

"Of course it does," Marike said patiently, "but not in DARDCO's computer. No one — not Sloat, not Alicia, and certainly not old Williams — can produce a copy of it. The only copy is now in my office safe, if you recall. And no one can demonstrate how reliably it works because the copy in ISAUR's computer has turned to nonsense."

"All right," Gail said. "I follow you so far. But how do we use the fact that DARDCO really doesn't have the program to influence the movement of the stock?"

"Well, that's actually the easy part," Marike said. "I'll call Lavinia Ott. She's a friend of mine and works at one of the wire services. She owes me a mighty big favor for bailing her out of a sticky financial mess a few years back. It would have ruined her career. I'll sketch the situation out for her. I won't mention your name, of course, but I will let her know that Sloat and company do not have this wonderful cavity location program after all."

Gail thought it over. "And then?"

Marike shrugged. "Then she puts the story on the wire. Because it's business news, it goes into the hard copy news telex system of every brokerage house around the world. And because it's *big* news, it will probably flash on every broker's computer screen. Within an hour of the news hitting the wire, DARDCO's terrific gains of the past few days will be wiped out. There'll be a selling panic.

173

And because stocks always fall faster and farther than they rise, the loss may be good for, oh, fifty points or so."

Gail listened open-mouthed. "How do you know all this?" she asked, amazed.

Marike blushed. "My father taught me a little bit about the financial markets. He was a pretty shrewd investor. And nowadays, thanks to computers, almost anyone with a telephone, a modem, and a computer, can get up-to-the-minute financial information, even in as remote a place as Bonaire." Marike was silent for a moment, staring into space, thinking. "You know," she said at last, "I've just thought of something else. There might even be a way for us to make some profit while DARDCO's stock is going down. It wouldn't begin to repay you for what you've been through, but with some extra money, you could, say, buy into a business here on Bonaire."

"Do what?"

"Buy into a business," Marike repeated, looking at Gail intently. "A SCUBA operation for instance."

Gail understood. Her eyes filled with tears. "That's a very sweet idea," she told Marike, "but I haven't any money to speculate in the stock market."

"Ah, but you won't need any," Marike said. "Not for what I have in mind."

"Are you serious?" Gail asked. "How on earth can you make money without spending any? And how can *anyone* make money from a stock that's declining? I thought the only way to make money in the stock market was from companies whose shares were increasing in value. You know — buy low, sell high."

"That's what most people think," Marike said. "But it's not true. No, we could do what's called shorting, or selling short, DARDCO's stock. It's easy. In effect what you do is first sell, and then buy. The same steps, only in reverse order." Seeing the confusion on Gail's face, Marike patiently explained. "Okay. Let's take oh, IBM, as an example. Suppose you'd watched IBM for years and saw it climb from fifty to its present high of about one hundred and seventy. You might well think that the time has come for IBM to turn around and head down again. And let's further suppose that you didn't own any IBM. What you could do is to sell short one hundred shares of the stock at current market prices — one hundred and seventy-three yesterday — and then wait for it to go down. Assuming you were right, the stock would then start to drop. Once it fell to, say, one hundred and twenty or so, you would simply buy it."

Gail shook her head. "I'm thoroughly confused."

"No you're not," Marike said. "You only think you are. What did you buy the stock for?"

Gail thought. "Well, one hundred and twenty dollars a share."

"Okay, and what did you sell it for?"

"One hundred and seventy-three."

"The difference?"

"Fifty-three dollars." Gail smiled. "But I have to multiply by one hundred, don't I? After all, I shorted a hundred shares of the stock."

"Bravo," Marike said, clapping.

"I still have two questions."

Marike groaned. "Trust a scientist."

"How can you do this with no money?"

"That was an oversimplification," Marike said. "Of course you have to have a brokerage account. And the account has to contain sufficient funds or shares of stock to support your eventual purchase. But for the first part

175

of this transaction, money doesn't go out of your account — it comes in."

"Because you're selling first, not buying," Gail said, nodding. "I understand. Now for my second question. Where do the hundred shares of stock come from? If I recall, you don't own them."

Marike exhaled heavily. "That's a good question. No, you don't own them. In fact you never own them. What happens is an internal brokerage account bookkeeping entry — your brokerage house either owns the stock, or borrows it on your behalf." She ran a hand through her hair. "Complicated, isn't it? My broker would be happy to explain the mechanics to you if you're still in the dark."

"Maybe someday," Gail said. "That's good enough for now, though. And you say this is done often in the markets?"

Marike nodded. "Pretty often. But if you don't know what you're doing, or if you're just plain wrong, you'll lose your shirt. If the stock doesn't go down as you'd planned, but goes up instead, your loss could be terrific. In theory, it's infinite. That's why short positions are closed fast. They're not conducive to sound sleep."

"I can see that," Gail said. "However, in the case of DARDCO, the downside potential looks greater than the upside, doesn't it?"

"Yes, it does," Marike said. "A lot greater. Well, what do you think? I know it won't be as satisfying as some other forms of justice — drawing and quartering, keelhauling, or maybe tar and feathering — but I have to tell you that nothing else has occurred to me." She shrugged. "And surely we shouldn't just sit here. I, for one, want to *do* something."

"So do I," Gail said. "But how could I possibly do it? I don't have a brokerage account."

176

"But I do."

"Oh, Marike," Gail said. "I couldn't do that."

"Why not? If it makes you feel better, you can borrow half the value of my account for the few hours this is going to take." She winked. "I'll even charge you an exorbitant interest rate. How's that for a deal?"

Gail shook her head. "It sounds too good to be true. Where's the catch?"

Marike shrugged. "Well, in the stock market nothing is a sure thing. As I told you, there's always the chance we could lose our shirts. Pardon me, my shirt. But I've risked my shirt on less likely prospects."

Gail chewed her lip. "You're the expert. If you think it's a good idea, let's do it."

"I'd like this to be our decision," Marike said softly, "not just mine."

"All right," Gail said. "With Sloat and Alicia out of the way, I'll be able to think about what I'm going to do with the rest of my life. All I can think about right now is that bloody helicopter landing on the beach." She looked steadily at Marike. "And with a little extra money, I might consider buying into that SCUBA business you were telling me about."

"I'm glad to hear you're thinking about it," Marike said quietly. "I want you to stay here, Gail. But I know what staying here would mean — a complete overhaul of your life."

"I'm not unwilling," Gail said. "Giving up marine geology isn't the hard part. I can live without it. What I've really enjoyed about it is working in and around the sea. If I had to give that up . . ." she broke off, staring at her hands. "I couldn't. But the chance you're giving me seems, well, a perfect compromise." She looked at Marike. "It's something I could do. And be happy doing."

She took a deep breath. "And I've been thinking about the cavity program too. If I could find an oil company that I could be certain would use the program in an ecologically responsible manner, I might sell it to them. I'd see that they used a big chunk of their profits to fund *real* underwater research, too. And to help clean up the oceans."

"We can talk about all that later," Marike said softly. "Right now let's see if we can pull this little stunt off."

Gail smiled. "So how do we do it?"

"Like this," Marike said, reaching for the phone.

Chapter 13

Gail awoke to someone shaking her. Startled, she sat up, rubbing her eyes.

"We did it!" Marike said exultantly.

"We did?" Gail repeated, trying to gather her wits. Hadn't it only been a few moments since she had left Marike staring at the green phosphor of the computer screen, gulping strong Dutch coffee to stay awake.

After talking to Lavinia, Marike had linked her computer to the *Dow Jones News & Quotes Service.* And then they waited. And waited. All sorts of interesting business news stories from around the world had flashed across the screen, but nothing on the cavity program. Finally, Gail couldn't keep her eyes open another minute. She would just go and lie down on the bed for a few minutes. The few minutes must have turned into hours.

"Why didn't you wake me?" she asked groggily. "I've missed all the fun."

"I called you two or three times," Marike said. "But I didn't want to leave the screen. The story came across, and then all hell broke loose. Boy, did that baby fall! Thirty points in less time than it's taking me to tell you about it."

"That fast?" Gail was stunned. "And did you . . . could you . . ." She couldn't think of a delicate way to put it.

"Make any money?" Marike supplied, laughing. She flopped down on the bed beside Gail. "Oh yes, we made money."

"Marike!" Gail exclaimed, delighted. "How much?"

"Just over a hundred thousand dollars. One hundred and three thousand, to be exact."

Gail gasped. "It's like . . . a fairy tale."

"That's a hundred and three thousand dollars apiece," Marike said off-handedly.

"Apiece?" Gail could hardly speak. "I'll never be able to thank you enough," she said shakily. "Never."

"I don't want you obsessed with how to thank me," Marike said, taking Gail's face in her hands and looking intently into her eyes. "Now you can do whatever you want. Stay here; go back to Erindale; go somewhere else. It's up to you." She kissed Gail's lips softly.

"I don't know what I want to do with the money. Or with my future," she said. "But I do know what I want to do right now."

"Oh?"

"Make love to you," Gail whispered, her voice tight in her throat.

In the dim light, Marike's eyes were enormous. "I was hoping you'd want to."

"I have wanted to," Gail said, bringing Marike's fingers to her lips. "But it hasn't seemed right before. Remember — I told you I wasn't very practiced at this sort of thing." She took a deep breath. "Well, that was a bit of a fib. In fact, I haven't had any practice at all."

"You worry too much," Marike said softly. "And as for practice, all the practice in the world can't take the place of feeling."

Surprised by the strength of her feelings, Gail pushed Marike back gently onto the pillows and leaned on one elbow above her. She traced Marike's eyebrows, nose, mouth, then bent to kiss her. She had meant to brush Marike's lips gently with her own, but Marike's lips parted and the tip of Marike's tongue quested for hers. Desire, smoldering until now, was suddenly red hot, burning. Gail was not sure who broke off the kiss. All she knew was that Marike's arms were about her, and it was she, Gail, who was leading them up to some unseen pinnacle of pleasure. There was never any question of not knowing what to do. Her hands found the warm skin under Marike's T-shirt, and Marike arched in pleasure, rising to meet her touch. Gail took Marike's breasts in her hands and kissed the nipples gently with her lips and tongue. Marike gasped, hands in Gail's hair.

"Oh God," Marike whispered. "That goes right through me."

Marike's growing passion fueled Gail's, and she found it almost impossible to go slowly, to concentrate solely on Marike. When she took one of Marike's nipples between her teeth, Marike's moan found its echo in her own white-hot stab of desire.

"Marike," she said, gasping.

"I know," Marike whispered, her voice ragged. "I need you to touch me, Gail. Now."

Gail ran her hands down Marike's body until her fingers found the soft tangle of hair between her thighs. Her fingers moved with an authority that surprised her as they slipped into Marike's warm, wet center, her thumb pressing the hard bud above.

Marike writhed, her hands tight on Gail's shoulders. "Please," she gasped.

Gail's fingers moved, beginning a rhythmic stroking, and she bent her head to kiss Marike's nipple again. Marike gasped as Gail moved her fingers in a quicker rhythm. Marike's legs tensed, then abruptly she cried out, arms flung wide as if in surrender to a pleasure too enormous to embrace. Marike's body shuddered, closing around her fingers in a series of spasms that gradually became flutters, then died away as her heartbeat slowed and her breathing became even.

"Was that . . . all right?" Gail asked.

Marike kissed Gail's palm. "That was indeed all right," she whispered shakily.

Gail put her head on Marike's shoulder. "I was afraid for a moment that I wouldn't know what to do."

"Didn't I say these things come naturally?"

Gail nodded, sighing. "Yes, you did."

"We'll have to see that you get more opportunities for practice," Marike said, yawning. "You're like an athlete who won't be happy until she perfects a new skill."

"You're right," Gail agreed, caressing the fine hair between Marike's legs. Marike placed her own hand over Gail's, and Gail was about to say something about the mixture of wonder and power she felt at giving Marike such pleasure, but she was suddenly too tired to say anything at all.

Chapter 14

The phone rang, waking Gail from a deep, dreamless sleep. She looked blearily at her watch. Almost three. Who could be calling at this hour? Sloat? Alicia? Had they realized where she must be hiding? Were they calling to taunt her? To threaten? Her heart rose into her throat and she sat up. "I'll go and get it," she told the barely awake Marike. "Stay here." She hurried across the cool slate floor of Marike's bedroom and down the hall into the living room. Moonlight shining through the windows cast fantastic moving shadows on the floor. Shivering, Gail looked apprehensively outside. A wild wind was lashing the tops of the palm trees into a frenzy — turning them into demonic shapes that weaved and thrashed like trapped things.

She grabbed the phone. "Yes?" she said groggily.

"Dr. Murray, it's Russ," a breathless voice answered. "Toshio and I are at Thomas' place, up near the road. He's hurt. Badly. Toshio's already called Dr. Hartog and Lieutenant Klee."

The bottom fell out of Gail's stomach. "Sloat," she whispered.

"Probably," Russ said. "Thomas didn't see who hit him. I just thought you should know about this," he said awkwardly, "in case you wanted to lie low or something until Lieutenant Klee gets here."

"All right," she said. "Thanks."

"Who is it?" Marike called.

Gail replaced the receiver with exaggerated care and made her feet carry her calmly back to the bedroom. Sitting on the bed, she brushed the blonde curls off Marike's forehead. "That was Russ," she said. "Someone just clobbered Thomas." Her teeth began to chatter. "It's Sloat, you know. I think he's on his way here." She closed her eyes for a moment, then bent and kissed Marike. "But he won't find me." Jumping to her feet, she hurried to the closet.

Marike flung back the covers and limped to her side, the cast making her slow and awkward. She took Gail by the arms and turned her around. "Listen to me," she said. "Sloat is finished. He can't do anything to you, Gail."

"How can you know that?" Gail asked, wanting to believe.

"Because I saw the decline in DARDCO's stock for myself. The stock closed down over forty points." She checked her watch. "And that was six hours ago. By now, Sloat had definitely gotten the word from his masters at DARDCO."

Gail shivered, and Marike put her arms around her, holding her close.

"But I can't just wait around here for Sloat to come marching through the door," Gail said. "I feel like a fish in a bowl. This house will be the first place he looks. And he *hurt* Thomas."

"All right, Marike agreed. "We'll go someplace safer until Rolf gets here. How about one of the boats?"

Gail took a deep breath. "Fine. But let's go now."

Marike pulled a T-shirt over her head. "Get dressed, then. We're going down to Osten One."

*****

Out on the dock, the wind was nearly unbearable. It whipped sand, bits of branches, and small stones into their faces, making it almost impossible to see. Clouds now covered the moon, and the only light came from the dim electric bulbs strung between the dock's pilings. As Gail watched, another popped and died, its glass shattered by flying debris.

"Wait," Marike said. "I want to get the rifle from the office. We're not going to sit on that boat like frightened mice." She ducked her head as a good-sized branch crashed against the office window. "Go on down to the boat and check the Whaler's lines. Watch your footing on the dock. It's going to be wet and slick. Hang onto the lines and be careful. Okay?"

"Okay," Gail said. Bracing herself against the boathouse, she tried to merge with the shadows. The dock swayed and creaked as waves surged against the pilings.

An occasional wave broke over the boards, drenching her feet, and she shivered in the cold, hanging onto the lines. She was terrified. Benjamin Sloat had taken on demonic proportions — he had become her childhood's bogeyman, her woman's fear. Incapable of clear thought, all she could do was follow Marike's instructions. They would simply wait on Osten One until Rolf came to give them the all clear. Sloat was just a man, after all, and only one man at that, Gail reminded herself, clinging to a rope-wound post as a heavy swell hit the pier.

Just ahead, Osten One bobbed in its berth, lines holding it securely against the pilings. She staggered from the shelter of the shadows across the boards of the dock, and stumbled over the side of Osten One and onto the deck. She checked the lines as well as she could, relieved that the knots seemed tight. The little cabin door was standing ajar, swinging back and forth, and she lurched toward it, ducking her head to clear the low doorway, reaching blindly ahead into the darkness.

"Hello, Dr. Murray," a woman's low voice said, a voice she knew only too well. The voice of Alicia Soto!

She opened her mouth to yell for Marike, to call for help, but she was grabbed roughly from behind, and a hand was clamped over her face.

She struggled frantically, trying to twist free, but her assailant held on tightly. She was breathing in sobs, unable to get control, hating herself for such weakness.

"Benjamin, you're having a terrible effect upon the good Dr. Murray," Alicia said, an icy amusement in her voice. "I can think of something a little more calming."

Gail heard a click, and then a light went on in the little cabin. She blinked, trying to focus in the sudden brightness. Before her stood Alicia Soto, arms crossed, a faint smile of satisfaction on her face. Her hair was pulled back and tied behind her head, and she wore a pair of jeans and a navy turtleneck. Gail was surprised at how different she looked, how unlike the woman she had seen at the press conference, how ordinary. She began to take heart. Perhaps these two could be beaten yet. After all, they were only two people. And Marike would be along any minute. With the rifle.

"Roll up her sleeve, Benjamin," Alicia said, reaching for a bag that sat on the cabin's little table. "And for God's sake, hold onto her while I do this. Then go out on deck and cast off the lines. Storm or no storm, we're taking our billion dollar asset out of here."

Gail's heart began to race. She would not allow Alicia to drug her again.

Still holding her tightly around the waist, Sloat removed his hand from her mouth. He put his free hand on her shoulder and pushed, urging her to turn around, loosening his grip. For one moment she was free. She pivoted, taking one step away from him, and drove a knee into his groin. His arms flapped, he made a gagging sound and fell away from her, stumbling against the table where Alicia was trying to load the syringe.

"You idiot!" Alicia yelled as he fell against her arm. "Stop her!"

But Gail had already reached the cabin door. Kicking it shut behind her, she staggered up onto the deck. This time she wasn't running away.

She fell to one knee as the storm tossed the Whaler against the pilings of the dock. Fumbling in the darkness, she found the compartment she wanted and yanked it open.

Behind her the cabin door was flung wide. She risked a look. A rectangle of light fell onto the deck, silhouetting Alicia Soto.

"Get back in here," Alicia told her. She moved a little and Gail saw the gun in her hand.

Fingers clumsy with fear, Gail finished loading Osten One's flare gun and snapped the barrel shut. "No," she told Alicia. "I'm not coming with you. I'm going to step off this boat onto the dock. And you're going to let me."

Alicia laughed. Bracing herself against the doorway, she brought the barrel of the gun up two-handed, to point at Gail. "Inside, Dr. Murray."

Gail heard the metallic *snick* as the revolver's hammer was cocked. She didn't wait to hear anything else. Holding the flare gun in front of her, she pulled the trigger. There was a popping sound as the flare was propelled from the gun's chamber, and a dull *whoomp* as the ignition process began. But there was no starburst of incandescence — only a dull explosion, and an instant of orange light, hardly bright enough to allow her to see Alicia's horrified face.

The force of the explosion threw Alicia off balance. She stumbled, half turning toward Gail as the boat gave a violent heave. Gail dropped the flare gun, hanging onto the rail with both hands. Alicia staggered three steps backwards, propelled toward the Whaler's high port rail. The rail caught her in the small of the back and she somersaulted into the sea.

For one instant Gail was tempted to let her go, to let the sea have her, to ignore her scream of terror. But she couldn't. Diving across the deck, she skidded to a stop against the Whaler's side and wrapped one arm and one leg around a metal upright. Bending over the side, she reached a hand down into the darkness. Ten feet below, the woman struggled in a trough between two waves, distinguishable only by the white blur of her face.

"Alicia — grab my hand!" Gail yelled.

Alicia raised one of her hands to Gail, but at that moment a wave took her. Gail could only look on in horrified amazement. It was as if the other woman had been seized by some sea monster — an immense black, undulating *thing* that bore her on its back, on a demonic ride from which there was no return. Gail heard Alicia scream again as the wave bore her past Osten One, and then she was gone. "Alicia!" Gail cried. "Alicia!"

Osten One rolled a little as someone jumped off the pier onto the deck. Struggling to one knee, holding onto a line, Gail turned in fear.

But it was Marike, rifle in one hand. "I couldn't find the bloody shells!" she cried in exasperation. "I thought I'd never get here. Which one of them was that?" she asked, gesturing at the water.

"Alicia Soto," Gail shouted over the wind. "She fell overboard. I tried to save her but I couldn't. Sloat's in the cabin." She covered her face with her hands. "This is a nightmare."

"Was," Marike said. She took two limping steps across the deck and locked the cabin door. "But the nightmare's finally finished," she said, putting her arms around Gail. "It's all over."

* * * * *

Marike's arm around her shoulders, Gail watched from the office window as one of Rolf Klee's men led Benjamin Sloat away. Slump-shouldered, dejected, he had no more fight left in him. Rolf nodded to them as he passed the window, and then they were alone.

"Rolf will come by tomorrow," Marike said.

Gail began to shiver. "I'll never forget the last glimpse I had of Alicia's face. What a horrible way to die."

190

"Come on, Marike said softly. "Let's go back to the house. What you need is food, drink, and bed."

"You're right," Gail said, taking a deep breath. The nightmare was over. She kissed Marike's cheek.

Marike peered outside. "It'll be dawn soon. And look — the storm's dying. Ready to brave the elements one more time?"

"Okay," Gail said.

Hand in hand, Gail matching her pace to Marike's, they hurried out into the gusty wind toward the lights that beckoned in the windows of Marike's house.

A few of the publications of
THE NAIAD PRESS, INC.
P.O. Box 10543 ● Tallahassee, Florida 32302
Phone (904) 539-9322
Mail orders welcome. Please include 15% postage.

OSTEN'S BAY by Zenobia N. Vole. 204 pp. Sizzling adventure romance
set on Bonaire. ISBN 0-941483-15-0 $8.95

LESSONS IN MURDER by Claire McNab. 216 pp. 1st in a stylish
mystery series. ISBN 0-941483-14-2 8.95

YELLOWTHROAT by Penny Hayes. 240 pp. Margarita, bandit,
kidnaps Julia. ISBN 0-941483-10-X 8.95

SAPPHISTRY: THE BOOK OF LESBIAN SEXUALITY by
Pat Califia. 3d edition, revised. 208 pp. ISBN 0-941483-24-X 8.95

CHERISHED LOVE by Evelyn Kennedy. 192 pp. Erotic
Lesbian love story. ISBN 0-941483-08-8 8.95

LAST SEPTEMBER by Helen R. Hull. 208 pp. Six stories & a
glorious novella. ISBN 0-941483-09-6 8.95

THE SECRET IN THE BIRD by Camarin Grae. 312 pp. Striking,
psychological suspense novel. ISBN 0-941483-05-3 8.95

TO THE LIGHTNING by Catherine Ennis. 208 pp. Romantic
Lesbian 'Robinson Crusoe' adventure. ISBN 0-941483-06-1 8.95

THE OTHER SIDE OF VENUS by Shirley Verel. 224 pp.
Luminous, romantic love story. ISBN 0-941483-07-X 8.95

DREAMS AND SWORDS by Katherine V. Forrest. 192 pp.
Romantic, erotic, imaginative stories. ISBN 0-941483-03-7 8.95

MEMORY BOARD by Jane Rule. 336 pp. Memorable novel
about an aging Lesbian couple. ISBN 0-941483-02-9 8.95

THE ALWAYS ANONYMOUS BEAST by Lauren Wright
Douglas. 224 pp. A Caitlin Reese mystery. First in a series.
ISBN 0-941483-04-5 8.95

SEARCHING FOR SPRING by Patricia A. Murphy. 224 pp.
Novel about the recovery of love. ISBN 0-941483-00-2 8.95

DUSTY'S QUEEN OF HEARTS DINER by Lee Lynch. 240 pp.
Romantic blue-collar novel. ISBN 0-941483-01-0 8.95

PARENTS MATTER by Ann Muller. 240 pp. Parents'
relationships with Lesbian daughters and gay sons.
ISBN 0-930044-91-6 9.95

THE PEARLS by Shelley Smith. 176 pp. Passion and fun in
the Caribbean sun. ISBN 0-930044-93-2 7.95

MAGDALENA by Sarah Aldridge. 352 pp. Epic Lesbian novel
set on three continents. ISBN 0-930044-99-1 8.95

THE BLACK AND WHITE OF IT by Ann Allen Shockley.
144 pp. Short stories. ISBN 0-930044-96-7 7.95

SAY JESUS AND COME TO ME by Ann Allen Shockley. 288
pp. Contemporary romance. ISBN 0-930044-98-3 8.95

LOVING HER by Ann Allen Shockley. 192 pp. Romantic love
story. ISBN 0-930044-97-5 7.95

MURDER AT THE NIGHTWOOD BAR by Katherine V.
Forrest. 240 pp. A Kate Delafield mystery. Second in a series.
ISBN 0-930044-92-4 8.95

ZOE'S BOOK by Gail Pass. 224 pp. Passionate, obsessive love
story. ISBN 0-930044-95-9 7.95

WINGED DANCER by Camarin Grae. 228 pp. Erotic Lesbian
adventure story. ISBN 0-930044-88-6 8.95

PAZ by Camarin Grae. 336 pp. Romantic Lesbian adventurer
with the power to change the world. ISBN 0-930044-89-4 8.95

SOUL SNATCHER by Camarin Grae. 224 pp. A puzzle, an
adventure, a mystery — Lesbian romance. ISBN 0-930044-90-8 8.95

THE LOVE OF GOOD WOMEN by Isabel Miller. 224 pp.
Long-awaited new novel by the author of the beloved *Patience
and Sarah.* ISBN 0-930044-81-9 8.95

THE HOUSE AT PELHAM FALLS by Brenda Weathers. 240
pp. Suspenseful Lesbian ghost story. ISBN 0-930044-79-7 7.95

HOME IN YOUR HANDS by Lee Lynch. 240 pp. More stories
from the author of *Old Dyke Tales.* ISBN 0-930044-80-0 7.95

EACH HAND A MAP by Anita Skeen. 112 pp. Real-life poems
that touch us all. ISBN 0-930044-82-7 6.95

SURPLUS by Sylvia Stevenson. 342 pp. A classic early Lesbian
novel. ISBN 0-930044-78-9 6.95

PEMBROKE PARK by Michelle Martin. 256 pp. Derring-do
and daring romance in Regency England. ISBN 0-930044-77-0 7.95

THE LONG TRAIL by Penny Hayes. 248 pp. Vivid adventures
of two women in love in the old west. ISBN 0-930044-76-2 8.95

HORIZON OF THE HEART by Shelley Smith. 192 pp. Hot
romance in summertime New England. ISBN 0-930044-75-4 7.95

AN EMERGENCE OF GREEN by Katherine V. Forrest. 288
pp. Powerful novel of sexual discovery. ISBN 0-930044-69-X 8.95

THE LESBIAN PERIODICALS INDEX edited by Claire
Potter. 432 pp. Author & subject index. ISBN 0-930044-74-6 29.95

DESERT OF THE HEART by Jane Rule. 224 pp. A classic;
basis for the movie *Desert Hearts.* ISBN 0-930044-73-8 7.95

MADAME AURORA by Sarah Aldridge. 256 pp. Historical
novel featuring a charismatic "seer."   ISBN 0-930044-44-4   7.95

CURIOUS WINE by Katherine V. Forrest. 176 pp. Passionate
Lesbian love story, a best-seller.   ISBN 0-930044-43-6   7.95

BLACK LESBIAN IN WHITE AMERICA by Anita Cornwell.
141 pp. Stories, essays, autobiography.   ISBN 0-930044-41-X   7.50

CONTRACT WITH THE WORLD by Jane Rule. 340 pp.
Powerful, panoramic novel of gay life.   ISBN 0-930044-28-2   7.95

YANTRAS OF WOMANLOVE by Tee A. Corinne. 64 pp.
Photos by noted Lesbian photographer.   ISBN 0-930044-30-4   6.95

MRS. PORTER'S LETTER by Vicki P. McConnell. 224 pp.
The first Nyla Wade mystery.   ISBN 0-930044-29-0   7.95

TO THE CLEVELAND STATION by Carol Anne Douglas.
192 pp. Interracial Lesbian love story.   ISBN 0-930044-27-4   6.95

THE NESTING PLACE by Sarah Aldridge. 224 pp. A
three-woman triangle—love conquers all!   ISBN 0-930044-26-6   7.95

THIS IS NOT FOR YOU by Jane Rule. 284 pp. A letter to a
beloved is also an intricate novel.   ISBN 0-930044-25-8   8.95

FAULTLINE by Sheila Ortiz Taylor. 140 pp. Warm, funny,
literate story of a startling family.   ISBN 0-930044-24-X   6.95

THE LESBIAN IN LITERATURE by Barbara Grier. 3d ed.
Foreword by Maida Tilchen. 240 pp. Comprehensive bibliography.
Literary ratings; rare photos.   ISBN 0-930044-23-1   7.95

ANNA'S COUNTRY by Elizabeth Lang. 208 pp. A woman
finds her Lesbian identity.   ISBN 0-930044-19-3   6.95

PRISM by Valerie Taylor. 158 pp. A love affair between two
women in their sixties.   ISBN 0-930044-18-5   6.95

BLACK LESBIANS: AN ANNOTATED BIBLIOGRAPHY
compiled by J. R. Roberts. Foreword by Barbara Smith. 112 pp.
Award-winning bibliography.   ISBN 0-930044-21-5   5.95

THE MARQUISE AND THE NOVICE by Victoria Ramstetter.
108 pp. A Lesbian Gothic novel.   ISBN 0-930044-16-9   4.95

OUTLANDER by Jane Rule. 207 pp. Short stories and essays
by one of our finest writers.   ISBN 0-930044-17-7   6.95

ALL TRUE LOVERS by Sarah Aldridge. 292 pp. Romantic
novel set in the 1930s and 1940s.   ISBN 0-930044-10-X   7.95

A WOMAN APPEARED TO ME by Renee Vivien. 65 pp. A
classic; translated by Jeannette H. Foster.   ISBN 0-930044-06-1   5.00

CYTHEREA'S BREATH by Sarah Aldridge. 240 pp. Romantic
novel about women's entrance into medicine.
    ISBN 0-930044-02-9   6.95

TOTTIE by Sarah Aldridge. 181 pp. Lesbian romance in the
turmoil of the sixties.   ISBN 0-930044-01-0   6.95

THE LATECOMER by Sarah Aldridge. 107 pp. A delicate love
story.   ISBN 0-930044-00-2   5.00

ODD GIRL OUT by Ann Bannon.   ISBN 0-930044-83-5   5.95

I AM A WOMAN by Ann Bannon.   ISBN 0-930044-84-3   5.95

WOMEN IN THE SHADOWS by Ann Bannon.
    ISBN 0-930044-85-1   5.95

JOURNEY TO A WOMAN by Ann Bannon.
    ISBN 0-930044-86-X   5.95

BEEBO BRINKER by Ann Bannon.   ISBN 0-930044-87-8   5.95
Legendary novels written in the fifties and sixties,
set in the gay mecca of Greenwich Village.

VOLUTE BOOKS

JOURNEY TO FULFILLMENT	Early classics by Valerie	3.95
A WORLD WITHOUT MEN	Taylor: The Erika Frohmann	3.95
RETURN TO LESBOS	series.	3.95

These are just a few of the many Naiad Press titles — we are the oldest and
largest lesbian/feminist publishing company in the world. Please request a
complete catalog. We offer personal service; we encourage and welcome
direct mail orders from individuals who have limited access to bookstores
carrying our publications.